HUNT FOR THE DEVIL MAN

THE 72 DEMONS
BOOK FOUR

JAMES E. WISHER

SAND HILL PUBLISHING

CHAPTER ONE

Daisuke Kugo speared a chunk of syrup-drenched pancake with his fork, the sweet aroma mingling with the savory scent of bacon. Sunlight streamed through the cafe window, casting long shadows across the table he shared with Helena. An extravagant assortment of breakfast dishes covered it from corner to corner. Ruq, invisible near Daisuke's right arm, only betrayed his presence when the occasional morsel of food vanished into nowhere.

Eager as he was to begin the hunt for Razak's prison, Daisuke had no intention of going into battle at less than his best, especially against the Devil Man backed up by a member—well, former member—of the Blood of Solomon. His first fight with the pair had made it clear they were not to be underestimated. Thus the need for a large meal to make sure he had enough energy.

Since when do you need to make excuses to enjoy a sugary meal?

He ignored Ruq's comment and grabbed a glazed doughnut. Before taking a bite he turned to Helena. "How's your magic?"

"Fully recovered." The beautiful blond wizard shot him a glare but it held no real heat. The cult of Abaddon had stripped her of her ability to cast for a little while and she didn't like to be reminded of it. "Do you really think finding the prison will be as simple as casting a tracking spell and following it?"

Daisuke shook his head. "Of course not. No one would be stupid enough not to neutralize such an obvious vulnerability, much less an experienced wizard like Remi. The truth is, I tested the spell this morning before I left my apartment and I couldn't detect the prison at all. I might be able to break through the barrier when we're closer, but I'm not counting on it. If this doesn't work, I've got a couple other ideas we can try."

"Care to share?" Helena took a sip from her steaming cup of tea.

"Sure. Rin says Vixen is recovering nicely." That bit of information brought a frown from Helena. She hadn't quite decided if Daisuke's decision to rescue the beautiful former assassin was a good thing or not. He hurried to press on before that argument could flare up again. "Assuming she's awake when we get back, I thought she may have some idea where Remi would run to. But option one is Vito. The Devil Man has been selling bound demons to criminal gangs. There might be some intel drifting around the underworld. The Italians owe me a favor, so they should be willing to share anything they know."

"I'm more worried about what sort of trouble the Blood of Solomon is going to cause," Helena said. "There's no way Vanessa will let what they did to her slide."

Daisuke glanced around the cafe but no one was paying them the least bit of attention. This was a known wizard hangout and everyone had better manners than to poke their nose into another wizard's business. It was basic etiquette in their world.

He blew out a sigh and finished off his doughnut. "I'm sure she won't. I kind of hope she finds them before we do and they kill each other. That would make collecting the prison so much easier."

More likely they'll make a deal and you'll end up fighting all three of them at once. Push the waffles a little closer.

Daisuke nudged the last two waffles over so his familiar could reach them. There was no way Vanessa would make a deal with Remi. The members of the Blood were all fanatics. Nothing could be worse in their eyes than betraying the cause. No, Vanessa wouldn't be satisfied until Remi was dead.

Helena's hand trembled as she set her cup down, her gaze darting between Daisuke and the table. Her brow was furrowed and she bit her bottom lip. "I won't slow you down, I promise. Despite what happened in Paris, I'm sure I can handle the mission."

"Hey, we're in this together. You've never been a burden and I'm sure you won't be this time." He reached out and touched her arm. "So let's not have any more of that kind of talk."

"Right." Helena exhaled, the tension seeping from her shoulders. "Together."

They polished off their breakfast. Well, technically Daisuke and Ruq polished off the breakfast. He didn't know how Helena managed given how lightly she ate. His magic drained so much energy that if he took in less than five thousand calories a day he'd start burning what little fat reserve he had. Once that was gone, he was screwed.

Their meal complete, Daisuke stood and tossed forty euros on the table. Ruq flew up on his shoulder and the trio stepped out into the bustling streets of Zurich. People hurried here and there, most on their way to work at this time of day. Work at a normal job where the fate of the world was in no way on the line should they make a mistake. Some days he envied them even as he knew a normal life would bore him to death in a month.

"Let's go." He set out for the nearest shadow. The Devil Man was waiting and it was time to begin the hunt.

R emi Velung strode into the Devil Man's sanctum. He offered a silent laugh at the name. The "sanctum" was little more than a glorified office. Much like the rest of this underground temple, it was a sad imitation of their former headquarters. Remi vastly preferred the space and comfort of Castle Ravenclaw. Of course, what he liked was irrelevant. When you were running for your life, any port in the storm was welcome.

Some nasty incense filled the air. It stung his nose and burned the back of his throat. How the Devil Man stood it he'd never understand. The room itself was filled with mystical junk. Fancy leather-bound grimoires mingled with relics made to look impressive by a variety of illusions lay scattered among parchments covered with gibberish scrawls written by some lunatic cultist from ancient times. It was the sort of collection designed to impress the ignorant, which described most of the followers of Abaddon.

And speaking of the cult, their leader, the Devil Man, an imposing figure swathed in obsidian robes, sat behind the desk. His hood was thrown back revealing the handsome face underneath. The man radiated charisma, unlike Remi, which explained why he was the face of the group. And it wasn't just the good looks and deep, sonorous voice. The Devil Man was clever and ambitious, a fact you forgot at your peril.

With a languid motion the Devil Man gestured toward the chair opposite his desk. "Remi, take a seat."

The words, softly spoken and slightly slurred, made Remi wonder if the incense had some effect beyond making the air smell foul.

Doubt etched deep furrows in Remi's brow as he paused to consider his options. Not that he had many. They were being hunted, both by the Circle of Sorcery and, he felt certain, his former comrades in the Blood of Solomon. There was no way Vanessa would let him escape after he betrayed the group, not to mention locking her in the dungeon of Castle Ravenclaw.

"Remi." The Devil Man's voice, as quiet as before, held a more demanding tone.

"Right," Remi muttered. He had to keep up appearances as the loyal second. Since Vixen's defeat, he had no allies save the cult. Only survival mattered for the moment. His own plans would keep for now. He took his seat, the leather creaking beneath him.

The Devil Man leaned forward, the candlelight from behind casting strange shadows across his face. "Remi, if we're to restore the cult and find a way to free Razak, we need more resources. The only place we can hope to get them is the gangsters who bought our demons."

Remi frowned and nodded. They'd discussed this before.

"I'm counting on you to convince them to provide those resources," the Devil Man continued, hands steepled before him.

"The gangs are likely to object since they paid in full for their demons already," Remi said. "What else can we offer them to sweeten the deal?"

"We can offer them their lives." The Devil Man's lips curled into a smile devoid of humor. "They're ignorant thugs. Tell them if we don't perform regular maintenance on their black rings the demons will break free and go berserk."

"That would've been more believable if we'd told them at the time of purchase." Remi was somewhat annoyed that he hadn't thought to do so in the first place. Such a basic source of ongoing profits was obvious in hindsight. Of course, he'd expected to have a greater demon under his control at this point and thus no need of anything else.

"Tell them you forgot to mention it." The Devil Man's dark chuckle filled the air. "They're so afraid of us they wouldn't dare argue."

"You might be right," Remi said. "But there are risks beyond the gangsters' reactions. Once I'm outside the wards, I might be detected."

"Doubtful," the Devil Man said. "They're tracking the prison, not us. As long as I keep it here with me, you should be free to move about as necessary."

Remi wasn't nearly as confident as his would-be master, but there was something to what the man said. At the end of the day, someone had to do something if they were going to move the project forward. The Devil Man didn't exactly blend in with ordinary society and the acolytes were too weak and stupid to intimidate anyone. No, it seemed it would have to be Remi.

Hellfire danced in the Devil Man's eyes when his gaze met Remi's. He leaned back in his chair, which groaned under his weight. Somewhere deeper in the temple the cultists began to chant in Infernal. It was distant enough that Remi couldn't quite make out what they were saying.

At last Remi said, "Fine. What will you be doing while I'm out risking my life for the cause?"

"Something only a hellpriest can do. You heard the chanting? When the preparations are complete, I'll contact Lord Abaddon and ask for guidance. There must be some other way to open the cursed prison and free Razak. If anyone would know how, the master would."

Remi wasn't optimistic on that point. If Solomon the Great hadn't figured out how to open the prisons without the seals, it probably wasn't possible. Still, couldn't hurt to ask, especially since it wasn't Remi's job. The idea of meeting a demon lord face to face didn't appeal to him.

He stood and said, "If I'm going, I'd best not delay. The sooner I get what we need the sooner we can summon reinforcements."

"That's the spirit," the Devil Man said. "I wish you good luck and may Abaddon bless your efforts."

Remi grimaced, but didn't comment as he turned toward the door. So far, the demon lord hadn't done much to bless their efforts and he doubted that was about to change.

❦

F lickering torches cast an uneven glow on the ancient stone walls as Vanessa Warhawk trailed a white-robed apprentice through the twisting corridors of Castle Solomon. The apprentice, one of the handful of youths who dealt with the mundane tasks necessary to maintain the castle while they studied to master their magic, led her toward the meeting room where Lord Solomon awaited.

Despite her urgency, Vanessa's gait was measured, even as her mind raced. Why had Lord Solomon delayed her pursuit of the traitor? Her magic had fully returned yesterday yet her request to begin the hunt was denied. Given the importance of finding Remi, she couldn't understand it. Not that she would ever question the wisdom of Lord Solomon. If he told her to delay, there was a good reason for it.

The meeting hall waited just ahead. It took all her self-control not to rush past her youthful guide. The apprentice knocked then pulled the door open, bowing as she gestured for Vanessa to enter.

She stepped into the room, her attention drawn to the figure seated at the head of the long table. Solomon the Great. His white hair and beard, perfectly combed, was stark contrasted against the tan fabric of the Robe of Power. His eyes were shadowed with dark ridges underneath. Whatever he'd been doing since she last spoke to him had taken a toll.

Solomon beckoned Vanessa to sit beside him. The chair scraped softly against the floor as she pulled it out. Vanessa took her place by his side. "You summoned me, Lord Solomon?"

"Indeed, Vanessa," Lord Solomon said. "I know you're eager to begin your pursuit of our wayward brother. I apologize for making you wait."

Vanessa's eyes widened. Had her impatience been so obvious? She cursed her foolishness. Of course Lord

Solomon had seen right through her. "Please don't apologize, my lord. My lack of patience is always a struggle."

"We all have our struggles. In any case, Remi has finally showed himself. I sensed his appearance only an hour ago."

A surge of exhilaration coursed through Vanessa. At last. She would be able to make up for her previous failure.

Vanessa frowned a moment later. "How did you find him, my lord?"

"A tracking spell utilizing the blood of Solomon we all share."

"I thought the link was too slight for such magic to work." The idea that Daisuke could hunt them down so easily filled her with dread.

"No need to fear." Again it seemed he'd read her like an open book.

Lord Solomon reached into his robe and pulled out a device from a hidden pocket. It looked a bit like a compass, albeit a crude one. There was a brass disk marked with the cardinal directions and an arrow made of some black substance she didn't recognize. The device sparked faintly in the ether, confirming its magical nature.

"It requires more than a simple spell to track us. This compass is one of a kind and amplifies the connection. As long as Remi remains outside whatever barrier hid him, this will locate him wherever he tries to run."

Vanessa accepted the compass, her fingers wrapping around the artifact as gently as they might an egg. The metal was cool, almost icy, against her warm skin. A moment later the chill vanished and the arrow fell so it pointed down.

"What happened?" she asked.

"I've set it to track Remi, but you have to provide the power to make it work. Simply channel ether into it and the compass will activate. As soon as you stop, it stops. Very simple."

So it didn't work on its own. Disappointing, but far from a surprise. Most magical devices worked the same way. She sent ether into it and the chill returned. A moment later the arrow spun back to its original heading, northeast.

"I swear I'll bring back Remi's head."

"No need for anything so dramatic. Just kill him and retrieve Razak's prison." Lord Solomon let out a soft sigh. "What we do is necessary, but also tragic. Remi has betrayed us, yes, and such treachery must be answered. But to hunt down one who is of our blood... It grieves me despite all he's done."

Lord Solomon was a better person than Vanessa. As far as she was concerned, Remi had died the day he decided to betray them. She was just burying the body.

"Good luck, Vanessa," Lord Solomon said.

"Thank you, my lord."

With the artifact clutched in her grip, Vanessa stood and left the meeting room. The teleportation chamber was waiting and beyond it, Remi. She didn't care who or what got in her way. No matter what she had to do, Remi would die and she would claim Razak's prison.

Heaven help anyone who got in her way.

CHAPTER TWO

Daisuke and Helena emerged from the shadow paths in an alley between the only two businesses in the village of Tamaz. The town's eerie silence always gave him a chill. There was a part of Daisuke that wanted to tear the place down. People shouldn't live in a place like this. The looming presence of Castle Ravenclaw cast a shadow over everything. Even abandoned, the castle held a dark presence.

Daisuke set Helena on her feet. Unlike Jinx, she lacked the power to travel through shadows on her own, which was why he had to carry her. Not that he minded holding the beautiful woman in his arms, but should it ever be necessary for them to escape in a hurry, it could be a problem.

A simple detection spell confirmed nothing living or demonic within his range. They might have been alone in the world.

"This place gives me the creeps," Helena said.

"You and me both," Daisuke said. "On the plus side, nothing's trying to kill us, so that's nice. I need to get the staff.

Keep your eyes peeled. There are ways to evade detection spells."

"Just because I got captured once doesn't mean I forgot how to do fieldwork." Helena's tone was sharp. Clearly she was still a bit self-conscious about her recent stint as a prisoner.

"You also almost got killed by Cristo and Itsuko not too long ago," Ruq said, not at all helpfully.

Hoping to end an argument before it began, Daisuke said, "Ruq, behave yourself."

The imp grumbled something unintelligible in Infernal before turning invisible. He and Helena had never gotten along, but this was a mission and they couldn't be distracted by pointless fighting. There would no doubt be plenty of the real kind soon enough.

Daisuke took out his wallet and removed a piece of metal about the size of a credit card. He charged it with ether then tossed it on the ground, where it transformed into a trunk which looked a little like a coffin. Buried under his clothes was a black staff made of gnarled wood, the Staff of Law, one of the three treasures of Solomon. The few smooth spaces on it were decorated with unique demon symbols. Those were the spots where he'd fused demon seals to the staff. Razak's was among them.

He returned the trunk to its card form and put it away. "Razak's prison is here somewhere. Let's see if I can find it."

He muttered the tracking spell, a simple one as such things went then charged Razak's seal with ether before sending the power back out. The resonant link should lead him right to the prison. "Should" being the operative word. As he expected, the spell fizzled.

"Nothing," Daisuke said.

"No surprise there, right?" Helena asked.

"Yes, but I don't have to be happy about it," Daisuke said.

"Maybe we should take another look around Castle Ravenclaw." Helena's voice held a tremor of fear. Her confident words aside, she was still on edge. Not that pointing it out would be prudent for him.

Daisuke considered for a moment. "No need to go back inside that hellhole. We need to find the Devil Man's escape hatch. There has to be a tunnel exit beyond the castle walls."

"Right," Helena said, a hint of relief in her tone.

Taking the lead, Daisuke used a spell to sharpen his senses as they walked up the road to the castle's front gate. It was a fair distance and passed through the nearby forest. It would be a perfect place for an ambush. Of course, to set an ambush you needed to know someone was coming. Daisuke could've appeared anywhere, making it difficult to anticipate his arrival.

Fortunately for them, his magic hadn't been deceived and nothing was lying in wait. A couple hours of walking brought them within sight of the castle. The ruined front gate looked exactly as he left it. Unlike last time, no claw demon came roaring out to attack them.

Twenty yards from the gate he turned right. They'd circle the wall and see what they could see.

"Ruq, take the high ground and let me know if anything catches your eye."

The imp launched himself off Daisuke's shoulder without a word of complaint. One good thing about Ruq, he always knew when to complain and when to shut up and do the job.

After a hundred yards of nothing save dirt and saplings Helena asked, "Do you think we'll find anything?"

"Sure." Daisuke's eyes never stopped scanning the ground.

"Whether what we find leads to their hidden lair is another question."

"If he knows we're coming after him," she said, tucking a stray lock of hair behind an ear. "Wouldn't he cover his tracks?"

"I'm sure he'll have made all sorts of efforts to hide his new base. The odds are we're going to strike out. But the arrogant prick isn't perfect. We may find something, though I doubt a wizard as skilled as Remi would be foolish enough to let a gap in the wards go unplugged. And if we don't, at least we'll know this avenue has been thoroughly covered."

"Are you always this methodical on a mission?" Helena asked.

"Depends on the mission. Sometimes you can skip a step or go right to the target. Though it helps if you know where the target is. When I'm tracking down someone who doesn't want to be found, it's best to go point by point. You never know which clue might be vital."

They continued their search, tracing the perimeter of the castle with meticulous care. This was the sort of tedious work Daisuke hated, but it was still better than a stakeout. At least he was moving.

A couple hours after noon Ruq's psychic voice appeared in Daisuke's mind. *Master, I see some disturbed earth about fifty yards ahead and to your right.*

That sounded promising. "Ruq found something. Let's take a closer look."

Following his familiar's psychic directions, Daisuke quick-stepped to the target location. Sure enough there was an area of freshly turned soil about six feet square. It wasn't a subtle thing. A blind man could've spotted it from a hundred feet away. The obviousness made him nervous.

Keeping well clear of the area, he looked closer. Sure enough, lines of ether ran through the dirt. Anyone who broke one would no doubt unleash a dangerous spell while alerting the Devil Man that his enemies had arrived.

"What's the holdup?" Helena asked. "A first-year rookie could disable that trap."

"True," Daisuke said. "And in doing so said rookie would be sure to let their prey know they were close. Not something I'm eager to do. What about you?"

She thought for a moment which surprised him. The answer seemed obvious to Daisuke.

"I'm not sure," she said at last. "If there was a chance of the Devil Man panicking, then it might be worth the risk to flush him out. The problem is, I don't know him well enough to say how he's liable to react."

"Fair point. I don't know him all that well myself. Ruq, come down here. You spent more time around the Devil Man than any of us. What do you think?"

The imp turned visible and landed on Daisuke's shoulder in rat form. "He won't panic. He's too arrogant. Besides, I doubt he has anywhere else to run."

Ruq's thinking meshed with Daisuke's. There was nothing in particular he wanted to see in the escape tunnel. Best to leave the trap alone and continue their search.

"I say we leave it as is and follow the tracks," Daisuke said.

Helena nodded. "Works for me. It's not like we can't come back later if we change our minds."

Daisuke rose from his crouch and led the way into the forest. The massive old-growth evergreens cast vast shadows which kept the underbrush to a minimum. That made for easy walking, but also a hard-to-follow trail. If the Devil

Man had been forced to smash his way through a bunch of saplings this would've been so much easier.

Though decent at tracking, Daisuke did the bulk of his work in cities. This trip, plus their mission in Australia had been unwelcome changes of pace. The idea that either the Devil Man or Remi could leave a trail this subtle struck him as ridiculous. Everything about the current situation felt wrong.

A few hundred yards into the forest Helena said, "This place gives me the willies. It feels like we're being watched."

"We are, sort of. Some earth wisps seem to have taken an interest in us. Don't worry, they're harmless."

"I've never heard of earth wisps. What are they?"

Daisuke stopped and looked her way. "They're the weakest sort of elemental spirits. Whenever you summon an elemental, a couple wisps sneak in with it. They like wild places without a lot of people. This forest is perfect for them."

"Did your family teach you about this kind of thing?" Helena asked.

"They taught me about all things spirit related. Fat lot of good it did—I still suck at spirit magic. Let's keep moving."

A tense hour passed before the trail ended. The earth itself seemed to swallow any hints of passage, leaving them standing in the middle of the woods, alone, with no idea where to go next.

"Damn it." Daisuke wanted to blow something up, but the trees hadn't done anything to draw his ire. "I knew that trail was too good to be true. A summoned spirit must've made it as a misdirection. Maybe the wisps snuck in with it."

He looked all around, stretching out with both his

magical and physical senses. If there was anything in the area, he'd find it.

But of course there wasn't. He found nothing but trees and dirt, neither of which he could question.

"Looks like we've hit a dead end," he said at last. "Unless you've got another idea, I think it's time we talk to Vito."

"Not Vixen?" Helena asked, the barest hint of annoyance in her tone.

"Last I knew she was still out. Considering everything the cult put her through, I don't want to rush her recovery. Vito, on the other hand, gets no sympathy from me. Jinx and I saved his fat ass and it's time for him to make good on his promises."

"Well, I've never been to Venice." Helena offered a smile that fell flat.

"The Venice you read about in brochures is a lot different from the Venice where we're going. The docks are about as romantic as a dog fight."

CHAPTER THREE

The Devil Man sat behind the desk in his office. The only light came from three black candles that were also the source of the swirling clouds of incense. Each breath he drew weakened his soul's grip on his body. The world was so hazy around him he could almost perceive the master's hell. Soon the time would come to cast the psychic projection spell.

Just as he drew a breath to begin the spell, one of the cultists pounded on the door. The solid thuds jarred him from the fragile psychic state he'd struggled to achieve. Two hours wasted. Whatever brought the fool to his door had better be important. If it were otherwise, he would happily cut the cultist's heart out as an offering to Abaddon.

The Devil Man's eyes snapped open, the once-hazy room now in sharp focus.

"What?!" he shouted. "What is so important that you dare disrupt my preparations?"

The door opened, revealing a young man who stood quivering in his boots, his dark robe trembling. Staring at the floor he said, "Master, the guardian spirits have reported an intrusion. Someone is searching the area."

The Devil Man snarled in annoyance. He'd known someone would be coming, but he hadn't expected them to arrive so soon. A good thing Remi had already left and put some distance between himself and the hidden temple. Had the intruder encountered Remi on his way out, it might have been a serious problem.

"Describe these intruders."

"There's a woman, pretty, with blond hair. She's dressed for the wilderness in boots and sturdy clothes. There's a young man with her, dark hair, jeans and a t-shirt. He looks Asian, I think; the view is blurry through the spirit link."

"Hmmm." He leaned back in his chair. The woman had to be one of his escaped sacrifices while he'd wager a great deal that the man was the wizard who'd forced him to flee Castle Ravenclaw. Hardly a shocking arrival. It was only a matter of time before his enemies returned. "They followed the false path?"

"Yes, Master."

Nice to know the diversion was working the way it was supposed to, though it was a shame the trap he left behind at the escape tunnel didn't kill them both. Well, you couldn't have everything. He knew that far too well.

"Go away." The Devil Man waved him back the way he'd come.

The cultist bowed, his hood falling forward to obscure his face even further in shadow, and backed out of the room. The heavy wooden door had barely started to shut before it was slammed open again. Another cultist, panting and wide-eyed, burst into the room, half tripping over his own robes in his haste.

"Master!" he said. "The strangers have disappeared."

"Disappeared as in the spirits can't find them or have they left the area?"

The man frowned and his brow furrowed. The question was clearly too much for his feeble brain.

"I don't know, Master, but I can't see them through the spirit link anymore."

He didn't care for the uncertainty, but unless something changed, he would assume they had left. There were plenty of other hidden spies. Should they appear somewhere else they would know about it.

"Well enough. Continue to keep watch, but do not disturb me again unless they breach the outer barrier."

"Yes, Master," the two cultists said in unison before closing his office door.

The annoyances had gone for now, but the threat was far from over. The Devil Man knew without a doubt that his enemies would never stop hunting him, not as long as he held Razak's prison. Let them hunt. This location was so well hidden no one who didn't know where it was would ever stumble on it. He had time and, Abaddon willing, soon he would have power. So much power no one would be able to stand against him.

Putting the cultists out of his mind, he settled back into his chair and took a deep breath of the spicy incense.

The Devil Man's mind stilled far more quickly this time and soon the office grew hazy once more. The ties binding him to his body loosened and when he felt the time was right, he began to chant in Infernal. The deep rhythmic words vibrated through the chamber. His heart slowed until it nearly stopped.

With a final, powerful command, he snapped the connection binding his soul to his body. A silver thread connected his foot to the top of his body's head. That link was his one way back. The Devil Man focused his mind on the flaming hellscape of Abaddon's home. Rivers of molten rock snaked through a barren land of scorched earth and smoldering ruin. Volcanoes belched plumes of sulfurous smoke, punctuating the sky with angry bursts of ash and flame. Amidst it all, the denizens of this domain reveled. Red-skinned hellfire demons cavorted in the crimson light.

In an instant, the vision became reality and the Devil Man hovered above it all. For a moment, he allowed himself to be swept up in the spectacle. One day, Abaddon's hell would be his home. But not today. Today, there was work to be done. And should he fail to perform it well, when the time came to join his master, he would endure suffering rather than inflict it.

The Devil Man shuddered. Best not to think too hard about that possibility.

Focusing on the most powerful source of corruption, the Devil Man willed himself toward it. Soon, the Hellfire Palace appeared in the distance, a massive monolith of black stone that rose out of a lake of lava, its many towers piercing the sky. No sentinels or demonic guardians patrolled the area. There was no need. Nothing could challenge Abaddon's absolute power here.

The Devil Man willed himself toward the courtyard. He'd barely begun to descend when an invisible force seized him. He was dragged along corridors hewn from the same black stone as the exterior, the surfaces gleaming with an inner fire. The halls were silent and empty.

He had no time to register anything more before he found himself flung into the vast throne room. A cavernous space, empty save for the Hellfire Throne, a giant black chair made of Hell-forged black iron. Upon the throne sat Abaddon in all his glory. A giant made of pure hellfire, the demon lord towered over the Devil Man.

Falling to his ghostly knees, the Devil Man prostrated himself before his master.

Before he could speak, Abaddon said, "Only the seal can free Razak. Your brethren in Europe have been hunted down until none remain. You stand alone, my hellpriest. Succeed and reap the rewards of victory, or fail and suffer the consequences."

The words struck the Devil Man like physical blows, each smashing apart a piece of his dream.

A moment later, the Devil Man was expelled from the throne room and sent hurtling back to the mortal world. He reentered his physical body with such force it left him gasping, his heart racing as it struggled to resume a normal rhythm.

He sat sprawled behind his desk, the smoke that had facilitated his journey now gagging him. With trembling hands, he reached out and snuffed the candles, leaving himself in total darkness. Darkness which mirrored what he felt at Abaddon's dismissal. He hadn't even received the honor of speaking to his master. Did the Lord of Corrupt Flames truly think so little of his loyal servant?

The answer was an obvious yes. Abaddon rewarded only success and the Devil Man had damn little to his name.

His hopes, it seemed, would have to lie with Remi convincing the gangsters to provide them with more resources. It was a dim hope, but far better than the alternative.

. . .

Remi soared, invisible, above the Romanian landscape. He was silent as a shadow above the train tracks that stitched the country together. Despite the weak central government, somehow the tracks were always maintained and the trains ran on time. It was as close to a miracle as Remi ever hoped to see.

Below him, a countryside filled with quaint villages, rolling hills, and lush valleys was a blur of pastoral beauty that Remi spared only a cursory glance. His mind was occupied with the task ahead. Bucharest was only a few miles away. Remi generally disliked cities—so loud and dirty. Still, when you needed to find a large group of criminals, there was no avoiding them.

Annoyance rose once more in Remi, a profound irritation with his role in the Devil Man's plan for rebuilding the cult's power base. He was a scholar and researcher, not a messenger. Even as the thought formed he knew it was foolish. None of the cultists could do what was needed and only the Devil Man could contact Abaddon. That left Remi as the errand boy.

He sighed. Reality could be cruel at times. Remi's lack of options had forced him into this position and if he wanted to survive and seize his destiny, he had no choice but to ride it out.

As the outskirts of Bucharest came into view, Remi set aside his pointless musings and focused. The sooner he finished running the Devil Man's errand, the sooner he could return to the safety of the hidden temple.

He descended toward a working-class part of the city filled with a mix of low-end housing and businesses. A dark alley struck him as a good place to land and as soon as he did, he released his invisibility spell. He blew out a breath.

Maintaining both invisibility and flight took a fair toll on him, though nothing that wouldn't recover as he walked to the gang's headquarters.

Remi stepped out of the alley and pulled up the hood of his sweatshirt. No comfortable robe for him today. He needed to blend in, so it was basic civilian clothes. He turned up the sidewalk and strode on, ignoring and ignored by the few people out on the streets this time of day. One of the advantages to this part of the city was the locals' understanding that excess curiosity could be bad for their health. If something didn't affect them, then it didn't exist.

Half an hour of walking restored Remi's magical strength and brought him to the gang's warehouse, a dilapidated structure that sagged in the middle. Lucky for them, winters tended to be mild as a heavy snow would probably collapse the dump. At minimum it didn't look like the sort of place the richest group of drug dealers in Eastern Europe would set up shop. The stink of mold mixed with the acrid bite of chemicals oozed from its cracked-open doors. It smelled worse than his alchemy lab during the nastiest experiments.

Remi marched right up to the door, making sure to give no sign that the stench bothered him. Any sign of weakness would set his efforts back and mark him as prey to the thugs inside. Remi was many things, but he was never the prey of weaklings.

He was a couple strides from the entrance when a burly man with a shaved head covered in tattoos stepped out to block his path. His leather jacket had polished spikes on the shoulders. Matching spikes decorated his heavy biker boots.

"We're closed. Piss off," the oversized doorman said.

"I'm here to see your boss. Tell Vasili the Devil Man sends his regards and that we need to discuss the black ring."

The doorman looked back into the dim warehouse interior then at Remi. You could almost see the gears struggling to turn in the man's brain. This was clearly a situation he hadn't been prepared for.

"Don't strain yourself," Remi said. "Just let me in so I can deliver my message. Idling out here is apt to draw unwelcome attention."

At last the doorman shrugged and pushed the door open a bit wider. "Your funeral, I guess."

Remi stepped past him into the gloomy interior. Crates stamped with shipping symbols and countries of origin filled a third of the space. Men loitered among the boxes, their faces scarred and angry. Tattoos snaked up their arms and often onto their faces. Their attire was a mix of leather, denim, and the odd flash of gold. Compared to this lot, Abaddon's cultists were ordinary.

At the very rear of the building, a table waited under a bare bulb. Seated at the table was a pale bald man in a fine blue suit. If there had been any doubt this was Vasili, the black ring on his right middle finger would've confirmed it.

Remi strode closer, ignoring the many hard glares sent his way. Ordinary thugs didn't frighten him in the least. He could kill them all with a wave of his hand.

Five paces out Vasili asked, "What have I done to warrant a visit from the Devil's Shadow?"

"Not a thing, Vasili," Remi said, his tone cool. "Unfortunately, it turns out we forgot to mention that the black ring needs occasional recharging. I'm here to make arrangements for your payment."

"Recharging?" Vasili shifted to look Remi in the eye. "No mention was made of such a thing when I dropped off your payment. This was supposed to be a one-and-done thing.

The ring and the demon for a hundred slaves. Now you're here looking for more?"

"Summoning and binding demons is a new field of magic. It's natural for us to discover new things about the process over time. Of course, if you're willing to risk your claw demon going berserk, that's your choice."

Vasili's face twisted. He knew as well as Remi what the demon could do since he'd sicced it on his enemies a time or two. No doubt he was now imagining what would happen to his men if it went out of control.

At last Vasili said, "How much and how often?"

Remi smiled. "Twenty slaves per quarter delivered to Castle Ravenclaw. Bring them yourself and I'll recharge the ring at the same time."

"You're a greedy son of a bitch, you know that?"

"Take it up with the Devil Man. I'm only here to deliver the message. Do we have a deal?"

"Yes, may you and your master choke on it." Vasili held out his hand.

Before their hands could touch, chaos erupted.

The warehouse door exploded inward, splinters of wood shooting across the room like shrapnel. All eyes turned toward the source of the intrusion. There, framed by the jagged edges of the destroyed entrance, stood Vanessa Warhawk, her figure outlined by the dim glow from outside. Her dark hair whipped about her face, the unmistakable white streak cutting through it like lightning.

"Vanessa!" Remi said. How had she found him? He'd only been out of the barrier for a few hours.

"Remi! I'm going to cut out your heart, wrap it in a neat bow, and bring it back to Lord Solomon." Vanessa slashed her hand through the air and half a dozen blue lines streaked out.

Two thugs were cut in half in an instant and Remi barely dove out of the way.

Vasili ended up under the table with him. "Friend of yours?"

"Hardly. Help me kill her and you can consider it your payment for six months."

"I would've killed her for the insult of attacking my warehouse. I'll take your offer as a bonus." Vasili raised his voice. "Whoever kills the witch gets a pound of gold!"

Gunfire rang out followed a moment later by the roar of Vasili's claw demon.

Much as he appreciated the gangsters' enthusiasm, Remi had no illusions about the odds of them defeating Vanessa. She was one of the Blood's more skilled combat wizards. Remi, on the other hand, was an artificer and researcher.

It was time to make himself scarce.

CHAPTER FOUR

Vanessa Warhawk made her way through the streets of Bucharest, the magic compass chilly in her hand. She'd traveled via the teleportation chamber to a town about fifty miles from Castle Ravenclaw. That had seemed like as good a place as any to start her hunt. And she was right. Vanessa had barely fed any ether into the compass before the arrow spun and pointed southeast, away from the castle. And from the strength of the signal, Remi wasn't too far away.

It was a good thing too since maintaining the flow of ether tired her out. Not horribly or anything, but enough that she could feel it. Taking to the air she flew south, pausing every twenty miles or so to take another reading. Soon enough she knew where the traitor was hiding. Bucharest was the biggest city in Romania. If you wanted to disappear, it was a good place for it.

Not that she imagined Remi wanted to disappear. He would've been hidden and safe had he stayed within whatever barrier had protected him. No, some goal had drawn him out of hiding. What that goal might be she neither knew nor cared. All that interested Vanessa was finding him and killing him in as painful a manner as she could manage. If she succeeded in torturing the location of Razak's prison out of him in the process, so much the better.

Vanessa shoved her daydreams out of her mind and focused. Around her, the city thrummed with life. From the clamor of vendors hawking their wares to the aroma of sizzling meat wafting from street-side grills, they were all background noise as Vanessa focused on her hunt. She side-stepped a chattering group of Brits, her eyes never leaving the compass's arrow. It pointed deeper into the city, away from the busy tourist area.

As she approached the warehouse district, the bustle of the city began to dull. The buildings grew short and squat, their windows grimy with neglect. The streets were littered with debris and the roar of diesel engines mingled with the cursing of teamsters. She'd visited plenty of worse places over the years, but she still had no desire to linger.

The compass arrow twisted to her left, down a narrow alley. She emerged on the far end facing the most rundown dump so far. The warehouse looked like it might collapse in a stiff breeze. In fact, the tattooed man standing in front of the door trying to look intimidating appeared sturdier.

Vanessa strode toward the rundown warehouse, her boots thudding on the pavement. She slipped the compass into her pocket. She had no doubt Remi was inside. He wouldn't escape her, not this time.

The thug outside leaned against the wall, lit a cigarette, and blew out a cloud of smoke. As Vanessa approached, he straightened, finally taking notice of her.

"Hey, sweetheart." He let out a wolf whistle before adding

a leer for good measure. "What's a pretty thing like you doing out here? It's dangerous in this part of the city."

"Is Remi inside?" Vanessa ignored his advances. She'd gotten plenty of them and no longer paid them any heed.

"Who the fuck is Remi?" the thug asked, blowing a smoke ring into the air.

Vanessa grimaced at the mingled stench of cheap tobacco and cheaper cologne. She needed to move this conversation along before she vomited on the sidewalk.

"He's a skinny little rat of a wizard," she said, her voice low and threatening. "Thinks he's the Creator's gift to magic. I know he's inside. It would be best if you moved aside then got yourself as far from here as possible."

"Ooh, feisty! I like that."

He couldn't say Vanessa didn't warn him. She raised a hand, her fingers splayed wide. His brow furrowed in confusion a moment before a fireball blew him backwards into the warehouse door and exploded, sending chunks of wood and thug flying in every direction.

She stepped over the threshold, her gaze raking across the interior. She took in the musty smell of old crates and the group of startled men, then her gaze settled on a table at the rear of the building. Remi sat there staring at her. Beside him was another man, this one wearing a fine suit. He was doubtless the leader of this outfit.

"Vanessa!" Remi said.

"Remi! I'm going to cut out your heart, wrap it in a neat bow, and bring it back to Lord Solomon." Vanessa slashed her hand through the air and blue threads of flame streaked out.

The spell cut two of the thugs in half but was a fraction too slow to hit Remi.

Someone shouted something in Romanian from under the table and bullets from a dozen guns came toward her. They pinged off her personal shield, causing her no more discomfort than light hail.

If this was the best they could manage, she'd burn her way to Remi in a minute. Threads of blue flame lanced out, slicing through men and crates with equal ease.

When the guns had fallen silent, a new challenger stepped out of the shadows. A demon, and an ugly one at that. Its ivory skin glistened with some kind of slime and, though vaguely humanoid in shape, it moved on all fours like a beast. Its hands and feet ended in six-inch claws that clicked on the cement floor. A guttural roar reverberated off the metal beams before it charged toward Vanessa.

Her threads lashed out only to fizzle against the demon's slimy skin.

A last-minute jump to the right saved her from getting eviscerated.

Fireproof, damn the luck. Hardly a surprise for a demon summoned out of Abaddon's hell. Pity for her that fire magic was her strongest. Well, she'd just have to adapt. Vanessa knew plenty of other sorts of magic. She'd have to hope something would be powerful enough to take it out.

The demon scrabbled around and sprinted toward her again.

Vanessa's hands moved in quick, sure gestures, conjuring chains of ice around the demon's torso and legs. They slowed it down for half a second before shattering into a thousand glimmering shards.

Vanessa grimaced and dodged another swipe of its claws. She'd hoped a demon that was strong against fire would be weak against ice. The problem was, she didn't allow for the fact that ice magic was her weakest element. She couldn't make the spell strong enough to penetrate its aura of corruption.

The demon lunged, and Vanessa leaped aside once more. The creature's claws gouged chunks out of the floor like the cement was putty. Vanessa was breathing hard. Between maintaining the compass on her way here and the spells she'd used so far, she was getting close to the end of her rope. If she didn't want to end up as demon chow, she'd need to think of something quick.

A sharp gesture summoned tentacles of lightning. They wrapped around the demon's limbs and sparked.

The creature howled and thrashed, threatening to break free at any moment.

She couldn't allow that. If it escaped now, Vanessa doubted she had strength enough to capture it a second time.

For better or worse, she had to risk it all right here.

Summoning every ounce of power she could muster, Vanessa sent a surge of ether down the tentacles. The demon spasmed and went rigid before exploding in a cloud of sulfurous fumes.

She'd beaten it, thank heaven. And no one remained to take a shot at her. Vanessa's stomach tightened. No spells had come her way during the fight. That would've been the perfect time for Remi to hit her from behind. Since he wasn't the honorable sort, it could only mean one thing.

She hurried over to the table as quickly as her battered body would allow and flung it aside. The man in the suit lay still and silent. Of Remi there was no sign.

A scream of frustration bubbled up in the back of her throat, but she swallowed it. Given her current state, his escape might not be the worst thing. Of course, Vanessa would never admit her weakness to anyone.

It took a few minutes for the worst of the aftereffects to wear off and when they did she kicked the unconscious man over onto his back. He didn't so much as flinch. The ring on his right hand held a lingering aura of corruption. It had to be tied to the demon and when it died he'd been knocked out by the backlash.

Vanessa didn't know how long it would take him to wake up and she wasn't inclined to wait to find out. She sent a tendril of ether into his abdomen followed by a weak burst of lightning.

He screamed and sat up, looking around with a dazed expression. Vanessa slapped him across the face, snapping his head to the side. That focused his attention where she wanted it.

"Let's make this quick," she said. "What's the deal with you and Remi? And more importantly, where can I find the little shit now?"

The gangster explained the deal he'd made with the Devil Man and that Remi, who he only knew as the Devil's Shadow, had come looking for more slaves in exchange for recharging the ring. "As for where he is now, I haven't the least idea. Though if you do catch up with him, I hope you kill him slowly. This mess has set my business back months if not years."

None of what he said rang false to Vanessa. Satisfied that he had nothing more of value to tell her, she killed him with a single thread of flame that sent his head to the floor with a wet plop.

Exhausted as she was, Vanessa had to know which way

Remi went. She took out the compass and charged it with ether.

Nothing happened. The compass didn't get cold and the arrow didn't move. Somehow the little worm had already found a way to hide himself. Vanessa swallowed another scream of frustration. There was no way she could fail now, not when she was so close.

She took a moment to calm herself. Remi couldn't hide forever, and when he showed himself, she'd be ready. Nothing would stop her from finishing things once and for all.

CHAPTER FIVE

The instant Remi saw that Vanessa was fully absorbed in the battle, he darted out from under the table he'd been using as cover and sprinted toward the rear wall of the warehouse.

"Where the hell are you going?" Vasili shouted after him.

Remi ignored the question.

He had no time to delay. It wouldn't take Vanessa long to deal with these fools, though he hoped the demon might at least buy him a little time.

The clatter of machine guns and the roar of magical flames nearly deafened him. He was a researcher for heaven's sake. The middle of a battle was no place for him. He cursed everyone and everything that had led to this moment starting with Solomon the Great and working his way down from there.

At the rear wall he searched for the door he knew had to be there. And found nothing. What kind of self-respecting gangster had a hideout with no back door?

Grimacing, Remi summoned ether into the tip of his

finger and drew a rectangle on the wall. A snap of his fingers released the gathered magic and disintegrated a quarter inch of marked wood. He shoved the makeshift door out of the way and hurried into the cool afternoon air.

Gasping, he pressed his back against the wood. He couldn't delay long, but a moment to catch his breath would be okay. It had to be given how his lungs were burning and his heart racing. A quick glance back through the opening he'd made confirmed the battle still raged. The gunfire had stopped, which meant the thugs were likely all dead. No great loss there. Hopefully the demon would fare better.

He shoved himself away from the wall and got moving again. He needed to think, but he could do it while he walked. He couldn't stop thinking about how Vanessa found him so quickly. He'd left nothing behind at Castle Solomon that could be used for a tracking spell.

No, he couldn't make assumptions. Solomon the Great might have some secret knowledge that would allow Vanessa to find him despite his precautions.

Remi had to assume the worst, that unless he took preventive measures, she would be able to find him no matter where he went. The thought weighed on him, making his weary strides all the heavier. Vanessa would never give up, not while she was alive. There was only one way to ensure his escape: a veil spell. It was complex and powerful and took the majority of his magical capacity to maintain.

But the alternative didn't bear thinking about.

"Damn the cost." Remi stopped and glanced around.

He'd lost track of where he was going, but perhaps luck had been watching out for him as he found himself in an empty part of the district surrounded by condemned warehouses. There wasn't a soul to be seen. Perfect. The fewer people who saw the veil activate, the more powerful the magic would be.

Gathering his will, he pressed his trembling hands together. His fingertips started glowing as the ether grew thick around him. With a whispered incantation, Remi wove the magic around him, blocking him from all forms of magical sight. When the veil finalized, he felt hollowed out, and a faint tingle at the back of his head confirmed he was on the edge of backlash.

He was confident in his casting, but he would only know for sure it worked if Vanessa didn't show up to try and kill him a second time. And if she did show up, Remi doubted he'd ever have to worry about anything again.

Protected by his magic, Remi resumed his grim march into the heart of Bucharest. He wove through the crowds, making certain not to meet anyone's gaze or do anything that might incite conflict. He was so reduced that even a small group of normal men might be enough to beat him. Or worse, force him to drop the veil and reveal his location to Vanessa.

The only hope he could see was to reach the home of the magical community. It wasn't an official district, but, in every city, it was there. He hoped to find someone capable of unraveling Vanessa's method for tracking him and, ideally, provide a countermeasure that wouldn't use all his power to maintain. Remi thoroughly disliked relying on others, but at the moment he didn't have any other options.

By the time he'd passed through the city center, Remi's legs were aching. If he'd known he was going to be doing fieldwork, he would've exercised more. At least he was close to the magic district now. The ether held hints of order, which could only mean wizards were nearby working spells.

Soon enough he found the turnoff, a modest side street that wouldn't draw a second look from a passing tourist, assuming said tourist wasn't a wizard. As soon as he emerged from the street, the area took on a different feel. The buildings were a patchwork of old-world charm and modern neglect, each brick a testament to the district's dual nature. It seemed the wizards in the area hadn't allowed the city to modernize the buildings.

He gave a little shake of his head. Some wizards had an unhealthy obsession with old things. He never understood it. You learned from the past, took what was useful, and updated it to make it better. Buildings were no different from magic in that regard.

Whatever. This wasn't his home and he couldn't have cared less how the people chose to live. For now, he needed to find a magic dealer. Though as he glanced around the district, he wasn't confident of finding anything suitable for his needs.

He passed shop after shop, checking their signs, and moving on when he didn't find what he was looking for. A few of the people out and about shot him hard looks. No doubt they could see the veil's powerful magical aura. Assuming they were skilled enough to recognize what it did, they were also likely wondering who Remi was hiding from. Better for their health if they never found out. He considered asking for directions, but preferred not to risk questions he didn't want to answer.

At last, after what seemed like an endless search, he found a little shop on the ground floor of a two-story brick building with a sign over the door featuring a potion bottle and wand, the ancient symbol of a magic dealer. With cautious optimism, he pushed the door open.

Remi stepped inside, the spicy scent of potions and dust striking him at once. It was a nostalgic smell that reminded him of his lab back at Castle Solomon. Then he remembered why he left and the good feeling withered. His eyes soon grew accustomed to the dim interior of the shop and he set to checking every shelf. Dusty amulets and charms sat here and there as if tossed at random. None of the trinkets appeared worth a second glance.

As he worked his way around the shop, Remi grew ever more skeptical. None of the trash on display glowed brightly in the ether. Even without a closer analysis he knew they weren't worth his time. Whatever faint hope he'd entertained was dwindling. Still, he'd come this far, better to make sure. Remi approached the counter where a crone stood staring at nothing with her milky eyes.

"Good evening," he said.

She jumped and snapped her head around to stare at him. "Who's there? My magic eyes see nothing."

"My name is Remi Velung," he said. "And my veil is hiding me from your magical sight. I'll have to ask you to forgive me for not lowering it."

"Ah, a veil. That explains it. If you're going to the trouble of casting such a potent spell, you must be in dire circumstances."

"Indeed, I am in a bit of a bind. Do you have an item that can mimic the effects of the veil?"

"Assuming I did, such an item would be expensive." She ran her gnarled fingers over the keys of the ancient cash register sitting on the side of the counter. "What have you to trade?"

This was the moment he'd been dreading. Remi was broke. But there was one thing he always kept in abundance.

"Secrets," he said.

"Secrets?" The old woman smiled, revealing her toothless gums. "How nice. Secrets are my favorite form of payment."

Exactly the reaction he'd expected. "So you have the item I need?"

"Let's hear what you're offering in exchange first."

Remi shook his head, his faint smile mirroring hers. "I think not. You'll get nothing from me until I can confirm the item does what you claim. Then, and only then, will we discuss payment."

The crone cackled. "I think I'm going to like you."

She turned to her right, drew a glowing square in midair, and stuck her arm inside up to the elbow. Extradimensional storage, not what Remi was expecting in such a rundown shop. When she pulled her arm back out, her hand grasped a golden shield broach which glowed bright in the ether.

Well, well, this had potential.

"Feel free to examine it. The shield amulet turns aside all scrying spells. Perfect for a wizard on the run."

Remi grimaced as he activated a simple analysis spell. It took almost no power yet still pushed him to the brink of backlash. Fortunately, it didn't take long to confirm that the item did what she claimed. It was pretty much perfect for Remi's needs. He made sure not to let any of his relief show as he worked. Not that she could see his reaction, but when magic was involved it was best not to take chances.

"This will do," he said at last. "What do you want to know in exchange?"

"Make me an offer."

Remi knew the perfect thing. "Have you ever heard of the Blood of Solomon?"

"Of course, everyone in the magical world, at least those who pay attention to such things, have heard of them."

"How would you like to know the names, descriptions, and abilities of every member?"

"I can think of several people who would pay dearly for such information. How have you come by it?"

"Simple. I am of the blood, but no longer a member of the group. We parted on less than friendly terms. Given the trouble they've caused me, the least they can do is give up their secrets in recompense. Do we have a deal?"

"We do indeed. Please proceed."

Remi took a breath and started talking. Hopefully the old woman would spread the Blood of Solomon's secrets far and wide. Nothing would please Remi more than to cause them no end of grief.

CHAPTER SIX

Vanessa left the messy aftermath of her battle behind and headed for the rear of the warehouse. Remi hadn't gotten past her, so that was the only way the miserable shit could've gone. The compass, once a reliable guide, now lay dormant and useless in her pocket. Whatever blocking magic Remi was using, it did a good job. But no matter, there were other ways to search.

It had to be taking a ton out of him to maintain such a powerful spell. That meant there was no way he could fly out of here. And if he couldn't fly, he certainly couldn't teleport or shadow walk. He had to be in the city. A city of a million people, but that was still easier to search than all of Europe.

A rectangle of light revealed a hole cut through the back wall of the warehouse. Bingo, this was where he went. Without hesitation, she stepped through the opening into the dim alleyway beyond. The area was devoid of people. Nothing like explosions and gunfire to convince the locals to make themselves scarce. Even in this part of the city, no one was hanging around to find out what happened.

Though she suspected the police would be along in short order.

All the more reason for her to be elsewhere. She just needed a direction.

Vanessa's gaze swept from side to side. Not a scrap of evidence betrayed Remi's direction, and no residual magic lingered to give her a hint. A quick check confirmed that the compass remained useless, its needle still and no sign of the magical chill.

"Son of a bitch," she muttered.

Where the hell had he gone? She calmed herself. Getting pissed wouldn't help her think clearly. Remi would no doubt be eager to flee the city. If he couldn't travel by magic, that likely meant the airport or the train station.

The station was closer so she headed that way.

Vanessa sat in the back of her cab and tried as hard as she could not to look at whatever was covering the floor. By some miracle the driver wasn't the talkative sort. Given her mood, if it had been otherwise she might have cut the tongue out of his head. Even better, the city's constant noise was reduced to a dull roar inside the car.

Taking advantage of the respite, she slipped the compass from her pocket and sent ether into it. The damn thing remained unresponsive, its needle swaying with the movements of the cab rather than pointing at Remi like it was supposed to. She had no idea what to do about it other than to keep checking every so often. The irony that Remi might well know what she needed to do to fix it wasn't lost on her.

She tensed as they approached the train station. The driver pulled up to a line of cabs and she tossed him a twenty-euro bill. Vanessa wove her way through the crowd, her focus total. She sidestepped a hurrying commuter then dodged a gawping tourist. The lively chatter and screech of trains was nothing but an annoying background buzz as she searched for the familiar, hated face.

After checking six platforms and finding nothing, Vanessa paused in the middle of the landing, drawing a string of curses from the running passengers.

"Idiot," she muttered. In her rush she hadn't been thinking straight. Remi wouldn't risk exposing himself by taking public transportation. The area was too open and there were security cameras all over the place. No, Remi would seek help among their own kind. "The magic district."

With newfound confidence and energy, Vanessa turned on her heel and headed for the exit. Every second wasted widened the gap between her and Remi. If she didn't catch him soon, he'd escape Bucharest and she'd have to start all over again, assuming she could even get the compass working.

A line of cabs waited outside the train station and she jumped in the first one she came to. The driver, a woman not much younger than Vanessa herself, asked, "Where to?"

"The magic district entrance."

The woman grimaced. "That's not a good place for regular folks like us to visit. I hear stories of the sorts of things they do there."

Vanessa summoned a ball of fire over her palm. "I'm far from regular folk. Get me within a block of the place if you're so scared. I'll walk the rest of the way."

The driver's eyes were so wide Vanessa could see the whites all the way around. "Please don't hurt me. I didn't mean anything by what I said."

"If I hurt you, I'd have to find another driver, a prospect that doesn't interest me. Just go."

The woman obliged, likely breaking a number of traffic laws in her rush to reach her destination. Fifteen minutes later she pulled off to the side of the road. "It's about a block ahead. No charge for the ride."

Vanessa had her faults, but she wasn't cheap. She tossed the driver a twenty and got out. Tires squealed as the cab pulled away.

She sighed and got to walking. Despite everything wizards had done for the world, they were still feared by some and hated by others. Lord Solomon always said that was the way of weaklings. Vanessa respected him above all the people she'd ever met, but sometimes his kind indulgence of regular people baffled her.

Putting the unpleasant encounter behind her, Vanessa turned down a narrow side street that ran into the magic district. Its cobblestone streets and antiquated buildings made a stark contrast to the steel and glass of downtown that she had left behind.

Vanessa took the compass from her pocket and glared at it. "One more time, come on."

She channeled ether into it. For an agonizing moment, the device remained warm and inert in her hand. Then there was a little chill and the arrow flicked from side to side, swiveling with jerky, uncertain movements before pointing directly into the heart of the district.

A moment later it went dead again, but that brief second of life had convinced her. Remi was here; now she had to find him.

Vanessa breathed out a long sigh and strode forward, deeper into the magic district. The first person she saw was a young woman, maybe twenty years old, wearing a simple blue dress covered with an apron methodically sweeping the front steps of a wand shop. Vanessa approached her, a fake smile she hoped would put the woman at ease plastered on her face.

"Excuse me," she said. "Have you seen a skinny guy with black hair dressed in a dark jacket and pants? It's very important that I find him."

The woman paused, leaning on her broom as she looked Vanessa over. "No, can't say I have."

Her tone was equal parts apologetic and indifferent. Not that Vanessa blamed her.

"Thanks anyway." Vanessa moved on, her gaze sweeping over the locals.

They didn't look much different than anyone else in the city. If not for the old-fashioned wooden signs advertising magical goods and services, it might have been any other tourist area.

As she walked, every few minutes she'd steal a glance at the compass. It was still twitching but it no longer pointed anywhere in particular. She assumed that meant Remi was somewhere nearby, but that's all it was, an assumption.

Her frustration grew as the compass needle continued wobbling without purpose. She pressed on, her eyes scanning the crowd for any sign of Remi's familiar narrow face or dark jacket. The magic district was quieter than most. A few tourists browsed here and there, but it was mostly wizards, both locals and those from elsewhere. The vast majority of ordinary people preferred to avoid places where wizards gathered. And for the most part the wizards appreciated their discretion.

"Excuse me." Vanessa approached a vendor peddling glowing charms from a cart adorned with nonsense runes. "I'm looking for someone—"

"Can't help you, love, sorry." He clearly wanted her gone so she wouldn't discourage the tourists from approaching and buying his tacky crap.

Not wanting to cause a scene on the off chance it might warn Remi, Vanessa gritted her teeth and walked away.

She barely managed ten strides before a voice called out, "You looking for someone?"

A street artist—she put the boy's age at about sixteen—decorating one of the buildings with glowing chalk, was waving at her.

Vanessa hurried over, pulse racing. "Yes, a slim, dark-haired man in a dark jacket and pants. He might have had a fugitive look to him. Does that ring a bell?"

"Yup. I saw a guy who looked like that pass by about an hour or so ago. My memory's a bit vague on where he went." The boy held out his hand expectantly.

She slapped a twenty-euro bill into it. "Well?"

He looked down at the bill and made a face. "Twenty? Are you kidding?"

She added two more and a warning. "Talk, before I decide to beat the information out of you."

The boy pocketed his bribe. "He went to the magic dealer at the end of the street. Two-story brick building. You can't miss the sign. Old Blind Malinda runs the place. She has to be pushing ninety."

"Thank you!" Vanessa didn't bother looking back. If the shopkeeper could give her a hint about where Remi was going, the sixty euros would be a bargain.

Vanessa found the place easily enough and burst through the door with a bit more enthusiasm than necessary. There were no customers. If Remi was ever here, he was now long gone. The shop's wares were a mixture of nonmagical junk and a few weak items of no consequence. She couldn't imagine Remi finding anything of real value here.

Vanessa marched up to the counter where a blind old woman in a black dress waited. "Malinda?"

"Yes, dear. What can I do for you?" The old woman's voice reminded Vanessa of her late grandmother. She found it soothing.

"My name is Vanessa Warhawk and I'm searching for a wizard. He's slim, dark hair and clothes." She studied Malinda's face, looking for a tell, a twitch, anything that might give away her familiarity with the name, but there was nothing.

Malinda tapped the side of her head near her sightless eyes. "Descriptions aren't terribly useful for me, dear. I did have one customer not very long ago and it was a man. Whether it's the man you're looking for, I can't say."

Vanessa cursed herself. Obviously the blind woman wouldn't react to a description. Her anxiety was making her careless.

"He said his name was Remi if that helps," Malinda said.

At last. "That's him. What did he buy? Where did he go? Anything you can tell me would be helpful."

Malinda's smile never wavered. "And why would I give away my customer's secrets?"

Vanessa's fist clenched. She'd never beaten a ninety-year-old to death before, but there was a first time for everything. "He's dangerous. You'd be doing the world a favor by helping me capture him."

"He's a wizard. We're all dangerous. Try again. Why would I give away my customer's secrets?" She made a point of emphasizing "give."

Vanessa relaxed. Of course, Malinda wanted money. This was a business, not a charity shop. "How much?"

"That's much better, dear. Five hundred, a magical item, or a secret. Your choice."

Vanessa didn't have five hundred euros on her and she needed the compass. That left a secret. She didn't know many and had no idea what sort Malinda would value. With a little shrug she said, "The cult of Abaddon learned how to fuse demons with masks, allowing men to transform into demons and retain their free will."

Malinda nodded. "Very interesting. Remi bought a shield amulet from me. As to his destination, he didn't say. The poor man seemed rather nervous about the person chasing him."

Vanessa clenched her jaw. A shield amulet would protect him from the compass's magic at no cost to his own power. It was the worst possible thing he could've found.

"That's not what I was hoping to hear," Vanessa said.

"The truth is often unpopular. Do you have any other business with me today?"

Taking the hint, Vanessa said, "No, thank you."

With that she turned and strode out of the shop. A quick look at the compass confirmed that it still wasn't working right, but it was doing something. Perhaps the shield amulet wasn't all powerful against tracking spells. She needed to contact Lord Solomon. Loathe as she was to admit it, Vanessa was out of ideas. If his wisdom couldn't get her out of this mess, she didn't know what she'd do.

CHAPTER SEVEN

Daisuke emerged from the shadow paths in a narrow Venice alleyway, Helena cradled in his arms. With his first breath the stink from the nearby docks assaulted his nose. Yes, they'd definitely arrived in the right place. He set Helena down and they walked out into the midafternoon sun. Across a nearby canal, dozens of warehouses lined a long road down to the waiting ships. Four huge cranes jutted into the air, heavy shipping containers dangling from their cables.

Looked peaceful enough. Of course, it had looked peaceful the last time he was here before he had to fight a bound demon and a bunch of guys with machine guns, so you couldn't always judge a book by its cover.

And speaking of nasty surprises... "Ruq, stay invisible and keep your eyes peeled. I don't want to run into anything unaware."

Like what? I can't sense any corruption and a few thugs with guns are no threat.

"Humor me."

With a bit of psychic grumbling Ruq launched himself from Daisuke's shoulder. The imp wasn't wrong of course, but it made him feel better knowing Ruq was on lookout.

"Do you think this Vito character will be able to tell us anything useful?" Helena asked.

Daisuke shrugged and headed for the bridge spanning a nearby canal. "I don't know, but if he can't, hopefully he can introduce us to someone who can. The underworld gangs have to keep track of what their competitors are up to, so I can't imagine they won't have heard about another group with a pet demon. Fingers crossed at least."

At the center of the bridge, Daisuke glanced down into the water. A fresh corpse chose that moment to drift by. He grimaced. The more things changed, the more they stayed the same.

"You were right, it looks nothing like the brochures." Helena stopped beside him and stared at the body bobbing face down in the murky canal waters. "When's the last time you took me somewhere nice?"

"Breakfast this morning?"

"That doesn't count."

"Australia?"

"There were werewolves and demons, not to mention Jinx. That doesn't count either. When this is over, we should go somewhere for a couple days, just the two of us."

"We'll see." Daisuke got moving again, leaving the corpse to find its own way. He didn't glance back but he doubted Helena was thrilled with his answer. He equally doubted their schedule would allow for that much away time. There was also Jinx. He didn't want to hurt the beautiful half demon's feelings by leaving her out. She didn't have many friends after all.

A little ways ahead of them waited a warehouse with the name Bombari's Import and Export written in large letters over its wide-open door. Outside, Vito, rotund and glistening with sweat like an eel out of water, shouted and waved his hands at the men unloading a truck parked a little to one side. Mingled English and Italian profanities hinted at the sort of person they were dealing with. Not that Daisuke needed any more hints to know Vito was a scumbag.

"Move your asses, you lazy sacks of..." Vito's tirade trailed off when he spotted Daisuke. A sheen of sweat glazed his bald head despite the cool ocean breeze.

"Didn't expect to see you again so soon, kid. And with yet another beautiful woman. Where do you find them? I'd like to pay the place a visit." Vito wiped his meaty hands on his stained shirt, leaving dark smudges on the fabric. He took a step forward and held out a now-hopefully-dry right hand.

Daisuke's smile held no hint of amusement as he shook hands with the man. "Vito. Quite the project you've got going."

"Yeah, I got a good deal on some new merchandise. And thank heaven for that. My wallet's getting awfully thin." His wallet was the only thing about Vito that was getting thin, but Daisuke forbore comment. "Somehow I doubt you're here to discuss my humble business ventures."

"You would be correct. We're looking for information about other groups buying demons from the Devil Man. You heard anything?"

Vito's brow creased with an additional wrinkle as he frowned. "Don't get me started on those bastards. I haven't heard a thing and if I never see another creature like that one you killed for us it would suit me fine."

"That's disappointing." Daisuke swallowed a sigh. It

would've been nice if Vito had an address for him, but heaven knew nothing ever went easily in this line of work.

"Don't look so glum," Vito said. "I said I haven't heard anything. But I know someone who might have. Don Luca. He's in town to oversee the cleanup of the docks personally. I told him all about you and he was eager for a meeting. If he knows anything, he'll tell you for free. The family owes you a lot."

Daisuke grinned. That was more like it. "You should lead with that next time. Where is he?"

"End of the docks, meeting with a potential client. Follow me." Vito turned to the workers. "You lot better have the truck unloaded by the time I get back!"

With that, Daisuke fell in behind Vito, Helena quiet beside him. He very much appreciated her willingness to take a back seat on this job. Technically she outranked him in the Circle, but if there was one thing the mob didn't like, it was dealing with women. They had some surprisingly old-fashioned beliefs in that area.

As they walked, Daisuke scanned the docks. Everything was calm considering it hadn't been very long since his fight with the demon. It seemed like there should be some people from the local security services at least. On second thought, he doubted the mob would want anyone looking too closely into the goings-on around here. And if they didn't want it looked into, you could be sure it wouldn't be.

He paused in front of the warehouse where the fight took place. The burn marks from his lightning blasts were still visible, but most of the damage had been cleaned up. Very quick and efficient. He admired that in an underworld organization.

"Keep up, Daisuke," Helena whispered. "Wouldn't want to lose sight of our illustrious guide."

"He's kind of hard to miss," Daisuke said. "I appreciate your patience with all this. The mob is basically a boys' club."

She shrugged. "I can't think of any women who would want to join. Don't worry, my ego's not that fragile. And remember, I've got your back whatever happens."

Some of the tension he hadn't realized he was carrying faded away. Though less powerful than Jinx, Helena was every bit as reliable. And while he preferred to avoid a fight if possible, he'd be glad to have her at his side should things go sideways.

They reached the far end of the docks where a small cargo ship sat moored to a quay, its rusted hull a testament to countless voyages. Beside it stood a middle-aged man, his black suit sharp, his hair oiled and slicked back. He gestured and spoke in a language Daisuke didn't recognize while a shirtless sailor whose skin was covered in nautical tattoos listened with a faint scowl.

Vito stopped a respectful distance from the pair. "We'll have to wait until the don finishes up. Shouldn't be long."

"What language is that?" Daisuke asked.

Vito shrugged. "Beats me, kid. The don speaks like a dozen of them."

"So he's a polyglot, interesting," Helena said.

"Best not call him that to his face." Vito wiped the sweat from his forehead and dried his hand on his shirt, adding another stain.

"It means someone who speaks a lot of languages." Daisuke didn't look away from the still-chatting duo. "I speak five and that was hard enough. I can't imagine learning a dozen."

The sailor nodded once before climbing the gangplank and disappearing onto the vessel. The man in the suit—Don Luca, Daisuke assumed—straightened his tie and turned to face them, a satisfied smile creasing his lips.

"Showtime," Daisuke said.

Vito took the hint and strode forward, his sweaty hands smoothing his shirt in a futile attempt at looking presentable. A few quiet words were exchanged before Vito waved Daisuke and Helena over.

Three long strides brought them face to face with the smiling mob boss. Don Luca held out his hand to Daisuke who gripped it. The handshake was firm, but he made no childish attempt to crush Daisuke's fingers. Dark eyes focused on Daisuke with almost uncomfortable intensity.

"Mr. Kugo," the don began, his voice rich with a faint Italian accent. "I cannot express my gratitude enough for your help in dealing with the recent... unpleasantness on our docks."

"Killing demons is what I do," Daisuke replied. "Glad to have been of service."

"Service indeed." The don released Daisuke's hand, offered Helena a polite nod, and continued. "Tell me, how might my organization repay such service?"

"I need information. The guys that caused you so much trouble aren't the only ones with pet demons. I'm hoping you can help me get a line on the others."

The don sighed and shook his head. "This used to be an honorable business. We had our battles, true, but they were fought between men not monsters. Not that the Serbians know anything about honor."

"Serbians?" Daisuke asked.

"Indeed, that's where our unwelcome visitors hailed

from. I have no knowledge of other groups playing about with monsters, but our information network is extensive." He paused, tapping a finger against his chin. "Give me a few hours. I'll make inquiries."

"That would be appreciated," Daisuke said.

"Excellent. Join me for dinner?" Don Luca extended a card with an address. "Seven o'clock. We'll discuss what surfaces."

"Sounds like a plan." Daisuke pocketed the card without so much as a glance. Another firm handshake sealed their temporary alliance.

As they walked away, Vito shuffled up alongside him. "The don took a liking to you."

"Good to know," Daisuke said. The notion of having a figure like Don Luca as an ally didn't thrill him, but the man would come in handy and nothing else mattered.

They dropped Vito at his warehouse where he got back to yelling at his help. Those guys had to be desperate for work to put up with him.

"We've got some time to kill," Daisuke said. "Want to have a look around the nice parts of Venice?"

"I'd love to see what the City of Bridges has to offer." Helena sounded eager.

"Then it's a date." Daisuke held out his arm and she grabbed it. In this line of work it was important to seize your moments of pleasure where you could. You never knew when it might be your last chance.

CHAPTER EIGHT

Jinx slumped onto her couch, the brand-new leather creaking under her. She was fairly sure this was the first time she'd sat on it since she rented the apartment. Her eyes glazed as the flickering light from the television played across the walls. She'd been clicking through the stations for hours but couldn't concentrate on anything.

It wasn't the shows' fault, it was her. Despite living for years alone in a cave, now that she had gotten used to company, she found being by herself was the worst thing ever. The key to Daisuke's apartment felt heavy in her pocket. She could go all the way up to his floor and watch TV, but it wouldn't matter. In fact, being in his apartment without him might be even worse.

She muttered a curse and flung the remote aside. It landed on the bare surface of her coffee table and skidded to a stop. The noise seemed far too loud in the small, nearly empty space. She stood and headed for the door. A quick walk in the fresh air would clear her mind.

A humorless smile quirked her lips. Who did she think she was kidding? At a minimum moving had to be better than sitting alone. At least she hoped so.

In the middle of the afternoon, the streets of Zurich were busy. Couples clasped hands, their laughter and shared glances forming a scene of contentment that Jinx wanted very much for herself. Of course, the person she wanted to share the scene with was far from here. She pictured Daisuke and Helena alone together and grimaced. That they were likely fighting for their lives rather than having fun did nothing to make her feel less jealous. Swallowing a sigh, she picked up her pace. As she feared, there was no relief to be found out here.

Maybe she could make herself useful at headquarters. Jinx turned toward Arcane Books and Trinkets, the magic shop that served as the Circle of Sorcery's base.

Twenty minutes later she turned down the alley that led to the shop's back door. She had her own key now and she used it to open the lock. A wave of her hand deactivated the wards and she stepped through into the now-familiar hall.

Jinx exhaled, the sound echoing in the emptiness as she locked the door behind her. She'd barely turned back when the boss's office door opened. The beautiful head of their leader poked out a moment later.

"Jinx?" The boss's golden eyes pierced her like she was a bug in a science display. "You're supposed to be at home resting."

"I tried to rest, but the apartment was so quiet and empty. Since I've had company, I find being alone difficult. I don't need to sleep for three more days and I can't concentrate on anything. You must understand what it's like. Fallen angels don't need much sleep either, do they?"

"We don't actually need any sleep," the boss said. "That's why I spend all my time here. I guess we can be insomniacs together." The boss considered for a moment, then pointed toward the staircase at the end of the hall. "Rin might need some help upstairs. Why don't you go see?"

Jinx didn't know Rin, the group's healer, very well. In fact, she was pretty sure she had only spoken to the young man once, when he looked over her wound after the fight with the hellfire demon. She wasn't sure what he might ask her to do—healing wasn't her area of expertise by any means —but any task was better than sitting by herself.

"Vixen is still recovering from her ordeal at Castle Raven-claw. Maybe a familiar voice will help draw her back to the land of the living." The boss must have mistaken her distracted thinking for hesitation. "She's the only patient at the moment, thank goodness."

Jinx didn't think her voice would be familiar since she never spoke with the woman. Still, she was happy to try. But first… "Have you heard anything from Daisuke?"

"I got a quick text saying they'd arrived in Venice and were on their way to speak to one of his contacts. The area around the castle was a bust. Daisuke and Helena are both fine."

Jinx relaxed a bit. He was okay, that was the most important thing. "Thank you for telling me. I'll let you get back to work."

Jinx climbed the staircase and tried to keep calm. She hadn't been this nervous fighting demons. It wasn't like she could screw up. Worst-case scenario, Rin didn't need anything and would send her back downstairs. No big deal.

She repeated the last sentence like it was a mantra and still didn't believe it by the time she opened the healing room's door. Inside she found Rin bent over Vixen, his glowing hands hovering just above her chest. Under different circumstances she might have thought he was up to something inappropriate, but he'd done the exact same thing to her when he analyzed her wound so she thought nothing of it.

Jinx stayed silent as she watched him work. Her half-demon nature prevented her from using healing magic. Even worse, if someone used it on her, it would work, but hurt like hell, pun intended. Lucky for her she seldom needed healing. Her nature ensured a naturally accelerated rate of recovery. Her stomach, for instance, was now healed without so much as a scar from the demon's claws.

Rin straightened and smiled, making him look even younger than his twenty-five years. "Jinx, what brings you by? Is your wound troubling you?"

"No, I'm fine, I just got tired of talking to myself," Jinx said, trying to make her tone light and failing miserably. "The boss thought I might be of some use up here."

Jinx took a quick glance at Vixen. Only her thin, pretty face and red hair poked out from under the covers. Her eyes were closed and her breathing steady. It didn't look like she was in any danger, at least not in Jinx's uneducated opinion.

"Help is always welcome," Rin said. "I just checked the flow of Vixen's life force. She's nearly ready to wake up. If you wouldn't mind sitting with her, keep her company so she's not alone when she comes around, that would be great. I've got a few odds and ends I need to do in the alchemy lab."

"I can do that," Jinx said. It was the perfect task for her, one she couldn't screw up.

"Great. If you need anything, I'll be right down the hall."

Rin hurried off to attend to whatever he had going on, leaving her alone with the unconscious Vixen.

"You're not going to be much help alleviating my loneliness," Jinx muttered as she settled into the chair beside Vixen's bed. Despite what she said, it did feel good to have a task, even one as simple as this.

The ticking of a small desk clock filled the silent room, accompanied only by Vixen's rhythmic breathing. Jinx watched the rise and fall of her chest, lost in thoughts about Daisuke and his dangerous hunt. She felt a pang of guilt for not being there with him. Foolish of course, if it had been her choice, that was exactly where she'd be. But it wasn't her choice and she had to accept reality.

An hour ticked by and Jinx was startIng to think she'd made a poor decision coming here when Vixen stirred. The groan she let out was so soft Jinx thought she imagined it, but when she looked, she found Vixen's green eyes staring back at her.

"Hey," Jinx said. "How are you feeling?"

"Okay, I thinI. Just weak." Vixen's hoarse voice was barely above a whisper. Her gaze settled on Jinx. "Do I know you? You look familiar."

Before Jinx could answer, Vixen's eyes got wide. "You were at the farmhouse. I saw you fighting a demon before the spirit made me kill those men and steal the prison. Where am I now?"

"This is Arcane Books and Trinkets," Jinx said, trying her best to sound reassuring. "You're safe here. Daisuke brought you back from Castle Ravenclaw. He's out right now, hunting the Devil Man."

At the mention of the Devil Man, a shudder ran through

Vixen's body, and her pale skin seemed to lose what little color it had.

"He's horrible, a monster that makes Master Remi look like a choirboy." Vixen shuddered and hugged herself under the blanket. "Will you stay with me?"

Jinx didn't hesitate. A fierce protectiveness welled up within her, unexpected but not unwelcome. "Of course I will."

Vixen pulled her arm out from under the covers and grabbed Jinx's hand. Her grip was weak, but determined. Jinx made a silent vow to do her best to help Vixen find her way forward. And maybe in the process find her own way.

CHAPTER NINE

Daisuke and Helena left the docks behind and headed for the nice part of Venice. The part where bodies didn't float down the canals but were scooped out before the tourists could see them. The little break seemed foolish when there was a demon prison out there in the hands of a crazy hellpriest, but they had no time to do anything else before joining Don Luca for dinner, especially since Vito was the only contact he had in the city.

Helena, by contrast, seemed delighted at the prospect of a little quality time alone. She held his arm in a tight grip and had a bright smile on her beautiful face.

They turned down a cobblestone street. A little ways ahead of them faint singing could be heard. Daisuke hated opera, but whoever it was had a decent voice. He guided Helena toward the crowd that had gathered at the edge of one of the canals. The source of the singing turned out to be a gondolier standing in the back of his boat. He bellowed in Italian as the crowd looked on.

You picked up a tail, Master. Two big guys in suits. Pretty sure they're armed.

Ruq's warning soured his mood. They were most likely Don Luca's men. At least Daisuke couldn't imagine anyone else sending men to keep an eye on them. His enemies were apt to use magic to hide themselves.

Are they wizards?

Doesn't look like it. If they are, they're really good at hiding their magical aura. They've also got guns, which I can't imagine a wizard bothering with. Want me to sting them to death?

Ruq sounded rather eager at the prospect. Pity Daisuke was going to have to disappoint him.

No. We don't want to antagonize the don by killing his men. Just watch them for now. If anything changes, let me know.

I never get to have any fun.

"What's going on?" Helena asked.

"Ruq spotted a couple guys on our tail." Daisuke kept his voice low. Thankfully the singer did a wonderful job distracting everyone.

Helena's eyes narrowed, a flicker of annoyance crossing her face. "The don's men?"

"I assume so. As long as they keep their distance, I'm inclined to ignore them."

"Agreed," Helena said. The gondolier fell silent and everyone started clapping. "Let's try the market. I've heard good things about it."

Daisuke shrugged. He wasn't feeling the date but didn't want to ruin Helena's fun. "Sure. It's a couple canals over."

The walk didn't take long and soon the noise of the Venetian marketplace filled the air. It made for a pleasant background as Daisuke and Helena went from stall to stall. There were food vendors, a woman selling silk scarves, and another crystal figurines. A stall selling flamboyant masks of all sorts caught his eye. He paused and ran his fingers along the contours of a mask painted with swirls of midnight blue and gold.

Grinning, he held it out to Helena. "For you."

She took it gently and held it to her face, giving her a mysterious air. "Thank you, Daisuke. It's beautiful."

He grabbed a second mask, this one black and edged with shadowy feathers. He paid the vendor for both then turned to find Helena frowning at him. "What?"

"Is that for Jinx?" Helena's tone was cool.

"Yeah. She was so depressed about not being able to join us I thought a little souvenir might cheer her up. Please don't be jealous. I told you before, I have no intention of choosing between the two of you."

Before the argument could really rev up, Ruq's telepathic voice said, *Two more suits joined the group. Still no wizards.*

"What the hell are they playing at?" he muttered.

"What's wrong?" Helena asked, all business once again.

"Ruq says our unknown followers have gone from two to four. I think it's time to find out what's going on."

"Where do you want to do it?"

"Somewhere with a lot less people."

They navigated through throngs of tourists and street performers, their pace brisk as they looked for a secluded spot. A park caught Daisuke's eye. It was nothing special, just a square of grass with a few benches. The main thing it had going for it was a complete lack of other people.

"This'll work." Daisuke summoned his trunk and put Jinx's mask inside, carefully wrapping it in one of his t-shirts. "Want to put yours in here? It'll be safer if there's a fight."

"Thanks." Helena wrapped hers up as well and he dismissed the trunk. "How do you want to handle this?"

"Directly." Daisuke took a deep breath and shouted. "Come out, or do I have to come find you?"

Silence hung in the air for an uncomfortable length of time until four men in matching gray suits stepped out from behind one of the buildings. They were stiffs, no question, but the bulges under their shoulders made it clear they were stiffs who took their business seriously.

"*Buonasera.*" One of them offered a smile that looked out of place on his rough features. The others stood silent behind him.

"So what do you guys need?" Daisuke asked. "You've been following us since the docks."

"Don Luca didn't want anything to happen to you before dinner tonight, so he ordered us to keep an eye on you."

"Guard duty, huh?" Daisuke didn't buy that for a second. No one with half a brain sent gorillas like these to guard a wizard. They were probably supposed to keep an eye on them and report back to their boss. "Well, we don't need guards, so you can split."

The lead Italian spread his hands in an apologetic gesture. "Signore Kugo, we mean no disrespect. The don simply wishes for your well-being."

"Thoughtful of him," Daisuke said. "But unnecessary."

"We have orders." The man's tone remained polite yet firm. "Our lives wouldn't be worth much if we disobeyed."

Helena muttered unkind things and he agreed with the sentiment, but the man's attitude made it clear that, short of violence, they were stuck with their unwelcome bodyguards.

"Fine," Daisuke said. It wasn't worth the fight. He checked

his phone. Only an hour until dinner. "Let's find a cafe. I need ice cream."

They left the park, the Italians trailing them at a discreet distance. The scent of brewing coffee and fresh pastries drew them to a little place overlooking a canal, but the usual allure of such pleasures was tainted by the presence of their new shadows.

"Great," Helena said as she settled into a chair. "Nothing says 'romantic afternoon in Venice' like being followed by mobster nannies."

"We were just killing time, remember?" Daisuke waved to draw the server's attention. He needed sugar and he needed it badly.

I want some too.

You need to keep an eye on our friends. I'll buy you a quart of double chocolate when we get home.

Half a gallon.

Fine, half a gallon.

And cookies.

Don't push it.

"What's he saying now?" Helena asked.

Daisuke grinned. "That he wants ice cream, what else?"

They talked about inconsequential things and watched the sun set. Daisuke enjoyed a vanilla gelato, while Helena sipped an espresso. With fifteen minutes to spare, the duo set out for their dinner engagement.

🏺

The gilded hands of an antique clock perched on the edge of the grand canal struck seven as Daisuke and Helena arrived at Don Luca's apartment building. They climbed the marble steps and strode through a gold-trimmed revolving door. The lobby was immaculate in a mix of polished wood, red velvet and gleaming brass. Daisuke pitied whoever had to clean all that.

There was a bank of elevators on the far wall, but only one had a pair of thugs in too-tight suits standing in front of it. These two looked like twins to the ones who had been following them all afternoon.

Daisuke led the way over, anticipating the familiar ritual of being frisked for weapons. To his surprise, the henchmen that greeted them merely nodded and pressed the call button. The doors opened and he and Helena stepped into the car. The ride up was accompanied by classical music, no doubt composed by some famous Italian guy now long dead.

The bell chimed and the doors slid open, revealing the penthouse suite's entry hall. It was all warm hardwoods and gold accents. Whoever said crime didn't pay was an idiot.

"Welcome." Don Luca's voice emerged from one of the doorways a moment before the man himself did. He had changed from his fine suit into an even finer tuxedo. Daisuke's t-shirt and jeans seemed completely out of place, not that he had anything to change into even had he been so inclined. "Please, be my honored guests this evening."

"We appreciate the invitation, Don Luca." Daisuke made sure to show the proper respect, not because he feared the man, but out of simple politeness.

"Just Luca, please. Neither of you is a member of my organization, so no need for such formality. Follow me to the dining room. Dinner will be served shortly."

The dining room featured a chandelier that dripped crystals like icicles, a table long enough to seat an emperor's court, and, if Daisuke wasn't mistaken, solid-gold plates. What sort of person wanted to live like this? Daisuke would've been afraid to touch anything lest he break it.

"Perhaps you could tell us what you learned while we're waiting." Daisuke pulled Helena's chair out for her then took the seat beside her.

"Patience, my new friend," Luca said. "A little indulgence might brighten your somber spirits."

Looked like Daisuke was going to have to play Luca's game if he wanted the information. It wasn't his preference, but he'd done things like this a time or two.

Servants emerged from the kitchen with the first course moments after they sat down, tomato soup and crusty bread. Daisuke silently cast a spell to confirm that there was no poison before taking a tentative spoonful. It was delicious.

Across the table, Luca stared at him, an expectant gleam in his eye. "Is it to your liking?"

"It's very tasty, thank you. Can you at least tell us if your sources turned up anything worthwhile?" Daisuke set his spoon down and took a sip of water.

Luca leaned back and smiled, clearly enjoying himself. "Patience, Daisuke. No need to sully such a splendid meal with talk of demons and darkness. However, if you were looking for a new job, I must say that my last wizard proved... underwhelming. I suspect you would be a far better replacement."

"No, thank you," he said without hesitation. "I'm quite content with my current employer."

The don's smile faltered, replaced by a tight-lipped frown. Daisuke doubted he was used to being so easily dismissed. There was no more conversation after that. The meal ended with dessert, a decadent tiramisu. It was as delicious as everything else. Through their link, Daisuke sensed Ruq's jealousy.

"The meal is complete," Daisuke said when the final servant had withdrawn.

"Fine." Luca let his exasperation slip out. "My contacts mentioned a drug ring operating out of Bucharest having a pet monster. The details were sketchy, but that's hardly a surprise given the time frame."

Daisuke stood and extended a hand, which the don grasped with a reluctant firmness. "I appreciate the info and food," he said. "We'll be on our way now."

Luca escorted them to the elevator. As soon as the door closed, Daisuke picked Helena up and stepped into the shadow paths. They needed to get back to Zurich and see if the boss knew anything about Bucharest.

CHAPTER TEN

Remi left the magic district via a different side street than the one he entered through. After maintaining the veil spell for so long he felt hollowed out. Between the battle at the warehouse and using so much magic, he was seeing double. All he wanted was a few hours' sleep. The shield amulet would protect him from Vanessa's seeking magic, so it should be safe enough to stop for the night.

The thought of Vanessa's relentless pursuit drew a grimace. He'd escaped her once, but he knew without a doubt that she'd never stop looking for him. The woman was too stubborn to quit. He dearly wished they'd managed to sacrifice her to Abaddon. She'd be much more useful to him as a corpse.

He staggered into a lamp post and cursed.

"Sleep," he muttered. Even a few hours would be enough to clear the cobwebs. A hot meal wouldn't go amiss either.

As if heaven was taking pity on him, he spotted the facade of a motel. The sign above the entrance flickered and buzzed, the exterior paint was peeling and the few cars in the lot looked like they hadn't moved in a decade. Not his first choice for a place to lay up, but the thought of looking for somewhere better made his knees weak.

Resolving himself, Remi pushed through the door. The musty odor that greeted him spoke volumes about the place. A bored clerk eyed him from behind the front desk, apathy etched deep within her otherwise youthful face.

"A room," Remi said.

The clerk reached behind her and grabbed a key off a row of hooks. "Sixty euros."

Bills changed hands and Remi took the key. The number four was engraved on the top. His thoughts were so bleary it took a moment for him to realize that was the number for his room.

The clerk took pity on him. "Out the door, turn right. They're all labeled."

He managed a weary wave of thanks as he trudged out of the office. The walk to his room felt like a mile but was probably only a hundred feet. The key protested as it turned but the lock did click open.

Remi stepped into the dimly lit room that now served as his temporary sanctuary. The curtains hung limp, too threadbare to block out the city lights. A nasty stink, a mix of stale tobacco and decay worse than the office, assaulted his nostrils. The carpet beneath his boots featured dubious stains which suggested a murder had happened not so long ago. And the bed, oh the bed. It was a sagging relic straight out of Remi's nightmares. Yet it was also the most beautiful thing he'd seen in days.

He considered once again, only for a moment, the possibility of finding another motel. Yet his legs rebelled at the thought. With a resigned sigh he accepted that, for tonight at least, this would be his new home.

After ensuring the door was locked and warded with a weak spell, Remi peeled off his jacket and made his way to the bathroom. The shower, thank the universe, was reasonably clean. He let the hot water melt the tension from his weary body. Remi had no illusions about his soul's fate, but if he somehow made it to Heaven, he doubted it could feel better than this.

Showered and bone weary, Remi dried himself with a spell, foregoing the dubious luxury of the motel's towels. He approached the bed, eyeing it with the wariness of a man who knew too much about the unseen world. A second, weak spell removed any bedbugs that might be crawling through the sheets.

Assured that no insects would feast on him tonight, Remi collapsed onto the bed. It groaned under his weight, but he barely noticed.

Minutes passed, but his mind refused to still. Instead of relaxing into sleep, it accelerated with worry. The shield amulet rested against his chest, seeming to weigh far more than its few ounces. Its presence was a constant reminder that he was hunted. With the power of the amulet, evading Vanessa would be simple, yet the fear of finding her lying in wait when he reached the next gang hung heavy in his mind. If she couldn't track him, that was the most natural next path for her to take.

Before he could do anything else, Vanessa needed to be dealt with once and for all.

As the minutes stretched endlessly, he searched in vain for a plan that would let him defeat the woman. Remi was under no illusions about the results of a direct confrontation.

She would kill him as easily as he did the bugs infesting his bed. He needed to trick her somehow.

The answer came out of the blue: Daisuke Kugo. He was as much an enemy of the Blood of Solomon as Remi himself. Could he convince the man to team up long enough to eliminate a shared foe? It was an interesting question and the more he thought about it, the less likely it seemed.

If not a team up, perhaps a ruse. If he could figure out some way to guide Daisuke and Vanessa to the same spot, nature would take its course. It was a dim possibility, but the best one Remi had come up with so far.

Having settled on at least a vague plan of action, sleep med him.

V anessa's cab skidded to a halt in front of the finest hotel in Bucharest. At least it better be since that was where she told the driver to take her. The twelve-story tower had a beautiful old-school design with gargoyles and spires to spare. When you were on a mission and it was possible, you needed to take advantage of such things. Given her recent dungeon accommodations, Vanessa was determined to spoil herself a little.

She strode through the revolving doors and took a deep breath of the lightly perfumed air. Her footsteps clacked on the marble floor as she made her way to the front desk. She was far from dressed for a place like this, but Vanessa felt certain the stack of euros in her bag would make up for her lack of style.

"Good evening," she said when she reached the reception desk. "I need a room for the night."

The clerk, a young man dressed in a black uniform with a sharp jawline and a gaze that lingered a bit too long on Vanessa's chest, smiled. "Of course, ma'am. Our rooms start at five hundred euros a night and that includes a free continental breakfast."

"That's fine." She counted out five hundred-euro bills and passed them over. Her brief visit to the ATM had been a good decision. The Blood of Solomon had provided her with plenty of funds in the form of a debit card connected to a dead-end bank account for this mission. She hadn't the least idea where Solomon the Great's fortune came from nor did she care. He'd dedicated all of it to the cause, a fact Vanessa greatly respected.

The clerk coughed as he stared at the pile of cash. No doubt most people paid with a credit card, but Vanessa had no interest in leaving a trail.

"Ah, right away," he said at last. "Your name?"

"Madam X."

He stared at her, then looked at the cash, and finally shrugged. His fingers danced across the keyboard and in a few seconds he produced a key card. "There you are, Madam. Your suite is on the twelfth floor. Enjoy your stay."

"Thank you." Vanessa took the card and headed for the elevator on the back wall.

As she moved toward the elevator, the opulent lobby began to fade into the background. Her mind was already racing to her next task.

She paused as she reached for the call button. Had she failed in her mission? She liked to think Remi's escape was just a temporary setback, but she couldn't deny that she'd reached a dead end. It shamed her to admit that she needed more help, especially after Lord Solomon gave her the unique compass.

Vanessa gritted her teeth and pressed the button. Her ego couldn't be allowed to stop her from completing the mission. If she had to ask for more help, so be it. Whatever it took to find Remi and the prison, she'd do.

Her mind made up, she stepped into the elevator and rode up to the top floor. Her room was only a few paces from the elevator. The suite's door opened silently when she swiped her card. Vanessa went inside, her gaze sweeping over the opulence. It was everything the dungeon hadn't been yet looking at it made the memories feel all the sharper.

She shoved the unpleasant thoughts away and pulled out her phone. Who should she call, one of the group's freelance associates or Lord Solomon himself? No sense bothering Lord Solomon if a contractor could help her. Smiling without humor at her justification, she pressed the appropriate contact.

Three rings and a bland voice devoid of accent and emotion answered. "How may I serve?"

"The artifact Lord Solomon provided to track the target has been rendered ineffective. Can you offer any assistance?"

"Negative. Our contract doesn't include magical assistance and I'm not a wizard in any case. I can search the web and attempt to hack the local security cameras to see if I can get a line on him, but that's it."

"Fine. Anything you can do would be appreciated," Vanessa said. She did her best to keep her disappointment from showing. "Call me with an update at seven AM local time."

"Understood," he said before the line went dead.

She sighed. No more delaying the inevitable. Another tap, this time on the first number in her list.

He answered after the third ring. "Vanessa. I trust you have good news."

"No, Lord Solomon, I don't. Remi has acquired a shield amulet and it's blocking the compass. I think. The compass is working, sort of. I'm not sure what to do."

"Describe exactly what the compass is doing."

She did so, making sure to leave nothing out. "Can anything be done?"

"Perhaps." She allowed her hopes to rise. "But it will be difficult."

"I've never been afraid of hard work, my lord. Please, tell me what I must do."

"Very well. It sounds like Remi's shield is imperfect. That means there are gaps in its protection. The compass is trying to force its way through those gaps. You simply need to give it the necessary power. Instead of pouring in just enough ether to begin the activation cycle, you need to overload it. Don't worry, even if you fed every drop of power you can muster into the compass, it won't break."

"I won't be able to maintain such a charge for long," Vanessa said.

"True. But it is your only option, at least as far as magic goes. If you can locate him via some other method, then by all means do so. As long as you succeed, the details are irrelevant."

"As you say, Lord Solomon. I will make the attempt in the morning. Right now, I doubt I have the strength to force anything."

"You know best what your magic can do. Trust yourself

and good luck. Should you need any more advice, don't hesitate to contact me again." He disconnected, leaving her alone.

Letting out a slow breath, Vanessa pocketed the phone. First food, then sleep. Rest would restore her strength. From the sound of it, she would need all she could muster to force the compass to obey.

Stepping out of her boots, she peeled off her sturdy trousers and blouse. Next she ordered room service and headed for the shower. Vanessa had no idea where Remi might be, but she hoped he was sleeping in a ditch somewhere.

CHAPTER ELEVEN

Daisuke emerged from the shadow paths in the alley behind Arcane Books and Trinkets with Helena in his arms. He set her down, fought a yawn, and failed. It had been a hell of a day, no doubt about that.

Don't forget you owe me ice cream.

As if there was any chance of Ruq letting him forget.

"I wish you didn't have to carry me," Helena said. "I feel like a burden."

"Having a beautiful woman in my arms is never a burden. Come on, I'm sure the boss sensed us arrive."

Helena smiled at his compliment. It probably wasn't enough to make up for their date in Venice getting screwed up, but it didn't cost him anything to sweeten her mood a bit. He went to the door and took out his key. It took three tries to fit it in the lock. He must've been more tired than he thought.

Inside, the familiar hallway stretched before them. As

they neared the door to the boss's office, it swung open and the boss stepped into the hall, her body surrounded by a haze of cigarette smoke. Her ash-gray suit was as immaculate as always and seemed to vanish into the smoke.

"I expected a phone call, not an in-person report," she said.

"There was nothing more we could do in Venice," Daisuke said. "And I wanted to sleep in my own bed. We'll head out again in the morning, assuming we can figure out where to go next."

"Come in and tell me about it." The boss waved them into her office.

Daisuke and Helena sat in front of her perfectly organized desk. When she'd taken her place behind it, Daisuke started talking. He went over everything they'd done since finishing breakfast with Helena chiming in here and there to add a detail he missed.

He finished up by asking, "So have you heard anything about Bucharest?"

The boss leaned back, deep in thought. "I have no contacts in the city government, but I do know an information broker that works out of the magic district. I can contact her and see if she's got any news. I'll have Crystal do a little digging as well."

"Sounds good, boss. I think I'd best head home before I fall asleep in your chair. What say we meet back here after breakfast?"

"There's one more thing before you leave. Jinx is upstairs. And Vixen woke up about an hour ago."

Daisuke grinned. "That's awesome. Though I can't imagine what Jinx is doing here. Wasn't she supposed to be home recovering?"

"She got lonely," the boss said. "I sent her to help Rin. Nothing too strenuous. Though I admit I feel a bit silly worrying. She seems fully recovered."

"Half demons are tough," Daisuke said. "Let's go up and say hi. If Vixen is up to it, I'd like to ask her a few questions."

"I'll stay here," Helena said, the annoyance tinging her voice again. "I'm sure you two would appreciate some alone time."

Daisuke rolled his eyes. What did she imagine they were going to do? "Don't be like that. I'm sure Jinx would be happy to see you too."

"No, I insist. Go have fun."

There was no way he was going to win this argument. "Suit yourself. I'll be back in a bit."

The staircase creaked under Daisuke's boots as he climbed. Three-quarters of the way to the top, Jinx emerged from Vixen's room and looked down at him, a bright smile on her pale face. Her red eyes seemed to glow brighter in the dim light. That was a sign of her excitement. As soon as he reached the top she hugged him.

"I missed you."

"Likewise. Sorry to leave you alone, I know you don't like it."

"True, but I'm not a child. I need to learn to adapt. Can you stay and talk for a little while?"

"Yeah, sure. But could we sit down somewhere? I'm beat. By the way, how's Vixen?"

"She's asleep again. Rin said it will take time for her to regain her strength."

Daisuke made sure not to let his disappointment show. He couldn't do anything tonight anyway. Hopefully she'd be awake by morning.

They moved the chairs away from Vixen's bedside and settled down on the far side of the room. Before the conversation could get too serious, Daisuke summoned his trunk and fished out the present he bought for her.

"Here." Daisuke handed her the black mask. "A souvenir from Venice."

Jinx's fingers slid across the smooth surface of the mask. "It's beautiful. I'll put it on the shelf in my apartment. Something to remind me of you when you leave again."

Gift delivered, he gave her a condensed version of his report. He found himself yawning every few seconds as he did. "I need to sleep. Are you coming back with me?"

Jinx's gaze shifted to Vixen, her expression hard to read. "I'll stay for now. Vixen is terrified of the Devil Man and Remi. I don't want her to wake up alone."

Daisuke nodded, surprised but pleased to see a real bond had formed between the two women. It wouldn't hurt for Jinx to have another friend in the city.

He got a goodbye hug and headed for the stairs. Helena was waiting at the bottom, arms crossed and eyes narrowed.

"What?"

"Figured you'd have company when you came back down. What happened?"

"Jinx is going to stay with Vixen. She seems genuinely worried about the woman. It was sweet. I'm going home."

By way of an ice cream shop.

"Yes, I didn't forget your ice cream." Now that he said it, Daisuke kind of wanted some too. "See you in the morning?"

"Breakfast at the cafe again? My treat this time."

"I like the sound of that." Daisuke kissed her on the cheek. It said something about how tired he was that he didn't try anything else. For the first time in a long time, he wanted his bed and he didn't feel like sharing. If the boss had any leads for them in the morning, he needed to be at full strength.

CHAPTER TWELVE

Vanessa stood at the floor-to-ceiling window in her plush hotel suite and looked out over the cityscape. The rising sun cast a golden glow over the urban sprawl. Her power was recovered from her exertions the previous day. She had rested well and enjoyed a delicious breakfast. A final cup of coffee warmed her hands.

She checked the clock. It was almost time. As if reading her mind, her phone rang.

"What did you learn?" she asked.

"Nothing." The contractor's voice was as emotionless as always. "Bucharest lacks an integrated system of cameras. What I could access showed no sign of the target. Your battle at the warehouse did draw a fair amount of media coverage, but no one knows any details about yourself or Remi."

That was about what Vanessa had expected, but having it confirmed did nothing for her mood. It was all down to the compass now.

"Very well. Continue to monitor local media for anything relevant to the mission."

"Understood." The contractor hung up.

With deliberate intention, Vanessa set down the coffee cup and took the compass out of her pocket. It felt heavier this morning. That was all in her mind of course. The weight was all mental. If she failed in this, she failed the mission. Vanessa refused to consider the possibility.

Closing her eyes, she exhaled slowly, centering herself and drawing ether into the compass. It flowed easily, confirming her full recovery. When the activation chill spread through her hand, Vanessa opened her eyes.

The compass's arrow was twitching, the same as it had the day before. Brow furrowed, Vanessa followed Lord Solomon's directions and poured more ether into the artifact. The metal soon grew so cold it burned against her skin, yet she held on, ignoring the pain and forcing even more ether into the compass.

Finally, the arrow halted, locking onto a direction somewhat between north and northeast. Triumph surged through Vanessa, but it proved fleeting. After only seconds her control of the ether wavered and the compass went back to twitching.

The room spun for a moment, but soon settled down. That had taken a good deal more effort than she expected. At this rate she wouldn't be able to check it more than once an hour.

Far from ideal, but at least she had a direction now.

Vanessa flexed her hand and winced. A ring of red skin covered her palm. It looked like frostbite. Not a surprise given how cold the compass got. She couldn't even use a glove since the artifact required direct physical contact to work.

Well, whatever. With any luck today would end things.

She pocketed the compass and called the front desk to arrange a rental car. Since she had no idea how long it might take to find Remi, having her own transportation struck her as a good idea.

An hour later she strode through the hotel's lobby. Outside, a sleek black sedan waited for her. Vanessa slid behind the wheel and fired it up. Pulling away from the curb, she used the car's built-in compass to orient herself based on the magical compass's last bearing. Pity it only gave direction and not distance.

Next she pulled up a map of the city using the onboard computer. Based on her direction of travel, Remi must have emerged on the opposite side of the magic district. Best to wait until she got at least that far before she checked the compass again.

Morning rush hour did nothing to speed her across the city, but she did make steady progress. Forty-five minutes after leaving the hotel, she was in what she considered the target area, a rundown section of the city bordering the magic district. If Remi was on foot, he wouldn't have gone far.

Hopefully.

Best to check and make sure she hadn't gone too far. Vanessa parked, took the compass out, and activated it a second time. The pain was worse, but at least she was ready for it. The arrow pointed due east this time.

She was getting closer, she could feel it.

Adjusting her course, Vanessa continued the pursuit. It didn't take long to spot the motel. The miserable, rundown dump looked like the perfect place for Remi to hide out. She glanced at the compass but didn't pick it up. It was too soon to check again. Weak as he was, if Vanessa wore herself out too much, even Remi would be able to defeat her.

No, patience would serve her best here. She found a parking spot with a good view of the motel and settled in to watch.

Nothing happened as she waited for her strength to return. When she felt ready, Vanessa took up the compass once more. The needle pointed right toward the hotel, directly at a door with a four on it.

"I've got you now," she whispered.

Vanessa stepped out of the car, ignoring the stink of rot and pollution. Her focus on the target was total. Remi wouldn't escape this time.

Halfway across the parking lot, the door to Remi's room opened and the man himself emerged. Their gazes locked for an instant before Remi turned and sprinted away as fast as his scrawny legs could carry him.

Snarling in frustration at the rotten luck, Vanessa ran after him. This wasn't how she imagined her final moment of triumph, but she felt confident that she was in better shape than Remi.

She would run him down like the dog he was and put him out his misery.

Remi groaned and rolled over on his cheap, creaking bed. Light seeped through the moth-eaten curtains, confirming it was time to rise and shine. His brain throbbed in protest as he hoisted himself into a sitting position. Despite a few aches and pains he felt mostly recovered, including his magic. Somehow he doubted facing today at less than full strength would end well. Not that he was optimistic about his chances at full strength either.

He forced himself to his feet and did a few stretches in hopes of working out the last few kinks. "Right then. Time to get started."

The problem was, he had no way to contact Daisuke. It wasn't like they'd exchanged phone numbers. What had seemed like a brilliant idea to his exhaustion-addled brain last night seemed far more dubious in the cold light of dawn. How could he have overlooked something so basic? Luring Daisuke into a fight with Vanessa would be a perfect solution to his problem, but how to go about it?

He paced around his modest room, boots scuffing the grimy carpet. Ideas flitted through his mind, each less practical than the last.

The Circle of Sorcery had to have a network of informants, just like the Blood of Solomon did. The busybodies were constantly showing up to stick their noses into things that didn't concern them. There was no way word of the warehouse battle wouldn't reach them.

He could use that.

The gnawing in Remi's stomach ended his deliberations. Food first. Once he'd filled his belly, he could sort out the details.

He shrugged into his jacket and strode toward the door. A wave of his hand dispelled the ward he'd placed on it last night. He'd half expected someone to try and break in. He had little enough worth stealing, but what he did have he wanted to keep. Remi was very much magic rich and cash poor. It was a common problem for men in his line of work.

He stepped out into the sun, squinting against the glare.

His gaze was drawn to a figure striding across the parking lot directly toward him.

Vanessa! How had she found him with his shield amulet in place?

Their eyes locked.

Time slowed for a moment.

Then Remi's survival instinct kicked in and he was off, sprinting down the street and away from the imminent danger that was Vanessa Warhawk.

He sensed an incoming spell and conjured a shield to angle it away from his back. An explosion five paces to his right made it clear Vanessa had no intention of holding back to protect the local population. Though given the state of this neighborhood, burning it all down might be an improvement.

It wasn't long before his breath came in ragged gasps. Running for his life wasn't something Remi often had to do, not before the last few days at least. Had he known the turns his life was going to take, he would've stayed in better shape.

More spells came arcing in, forcing him to expend energy turning them aside. The only good thing about his current situation was that it took way more power to attack than it did to defend. Especially if, like Remi, you didn't care where they ended up going off.

He barreled past startled faces staring out from alleys or the windows of parked cars. Speaking of cars, one of them exploded far too close for comfort.

Screams were soon added to the soundtrack of his head-long flight. Men and women rushed to get out of the line of fire. Some with greater success than others. Remi ignored them all. Only one life interested him and it didn't belong to a random bum in the Bucharest slums.

Skidding around a corner, Remi spotted potential salvation, an idling police car. Loud music came from the vehicle and the two men inside were nodding along to the beat. Could these fools not hear what was going on?

Well, he'd sort that out shortly.

"Help!" he screamed and waved his hands. "Help!"

The two officers jerked to attention, leapt out of the car, hands reaching for their pistols as they stared at the scene before them.

"She's trying to kill me!" Remi shouted then waved toward the smoke rising behind him.

He'd barely finished speaking when Vanessa rounded the bend, eyes narrowed in lethal fury and flames dancing around her hands.

The officers needed no more convincing. They turned their guns on Vanessa and opened fire. Bullets pinged off of her shield, drawing a grimace.

Remi needed less than a second to take all that in and then he was moving again. He bolted past the police car and offered a silent prayer that the useless idiots could buy him at least a minute or two.

He didn't know how far he got before the pain in his lungs forced him to stop. In the shade of an overpass, Remi's breath came in ragged gasps. The acrid stench of exhaust burned his throat, but he couldn't slow his breathing. He saw no sign of Vanessa but harbored no illusions about his escape. It was temporary at best.

When he got himself under control, the roar of engines caught his attention. It was coming from further down the street. The last thing he wanted to do was walk some more, but he couldn't stand around and wait for his pursuer to catch up.

He pushed away from the concrete pillar he'd been leaning on and followed the roar. Soon enough he found a dozen bikers, their motorcycles growling, beside the rusted fence of a basketball court. They were a rough-looking bunch, lots of leather and tattoos. Remi cared not in the least about their looks. Only the bikes interested him. They were his way to put some distance between himself and Vanessa. That he couldn't drive one was a problem easily solved by a little psychic domination.

Mind made up, he marched across the street. The bikers' grins widened at his approach, mistaking his slender form and disheveled state for weakness. He might not be a match for Vanessa, but he could handle this lot without breaking a sweat.

"Good evening, gentlemen," Remi said. "I'd love to take one of your bikes for a ride."

They roared with laughter just as he expected them to. They were too stupid and arrogant to recognize danger when it stood right in front of them.

Much as Remi would've enjoyed playing with these fools, he had no time today. A snap of his fingers combined with a sharp incantation sent blades of ether lashing out, severing heads and limbs with equal ease.

The lone survivor, a behemoth of a man whose terror-stricken eyes were filled with tears when they met Remi's, said, "Please. I'll do anything you want. Just don't kill me."

"I appreciate your attitude. Take me to the warehouse district. Try anything funny and I'll peel you like an apple. Understand?"

The survivor nodded, scrambling to his feet, and guided Remi toward a large black-and-chrome chopper. He slung his leg over the seat and Remi climbed up behind him. A moment later they were roaring down the street away from Vanessa and hopefully toward Daisuke.

CHAPTER THIRTEEN

Daisuke and Helena approached the back door of Arcane Books and Trinkets after enjoying ale meal at the cafe. A good night's sleep and food had left Daisuke restored and ready to resume the hunt for Razak's prison. With any luck Crystal and the boss had worked their magic and found him some leads. If not, he was going to have to risk talking to Vixen and, based on what Jinx said, the conversation would be awfully traumatic for the woman. Given all she'd been through, Daisuke would prefer to avoid adding to her stress.

"What do you think?" Helena asked. Didn't sound like she was still pissed about him hanging out with Jinx yesterday. That was good. He hated dealing with Helena when she was in a mood.

"I don't know. Making progress around Castle Ravenclaw seems unlikely. I'd prefer not to stress Vixen out any further. Hopefully the boss has something we can follow up on."

He opened the door and held it for Helena then followed her inside. The shop hadn't opened for the day yet so everything was quiet. They turned down the hall to the boss's office. Daisuke knocked, but the only response was silence.

Weird, usually she called them right in. He concentrated and sure enough her divine presence was inside. The boss used to make an effort to mask her aura, but since they'd learned her secret, that she was really Angelique, a fallen angel, she didn't bother anymore.

"What do you think she's doing?" Helena asked.

Daisuke shrugged. He hadn't the least idea.

After a long five minutes the boss said, "Come in."

Daisuke opened the door and she waved them into the chairs in front of her desk. As far as he could tell she was wearing the same gray suit as the night before. Of course, all her suits looked the same, so it was hard to say for sure.

"Everything okay?" Daisuke asked.

"More or less. I was on the phone with my contact in Bucharest. Both Remi and Vanessa paid her shop a visit which confirms they're both in the city."

"That's good news, right?" Daisuke asked.

The boss flicked ash from her cigarette into an over-loaded ashtray. "Good for us, but maybe bad for Bucharest. Crystal's been busy too. Turns out a warehouse owned by a notorious drug dealer became an arena for a sorcerous battle. Over a dozen killed. I doubt that's a coincidence."

"What do you want to bet this is the same gang Don Luca said bought a demon from Remi?" Helena said.

"No bet," Daisuke said. "Odds are Remi's calling in favors as the cult of Abaddon tries to rebuild. I wonder how Vanessa found him."

"According to Malinda," the boss said. "Remi bought a shield amulet. That means Vanessa must have some way to track him. Not at all impossible given the Blood of

Solomon's resources. In any case, you two need to go to Bucharest and deal with both of them before any more people die."

"I've never visited Bucharest," Daisuke said. "We'll have to detour via Tamaz, then fly south. Shouldn't take more than an hour. Will we be working with the police or do we need to stay on the down-low?"

"Regrettably, my network doesn't include anyone in their security forces, so you'll be on your own. Try to keep the damage to a minimum."

"I always try, but the other team has a say in how it goes." Daisuke shrugged in a "what can you do?" gesture.

"Also, while you're there, talk to Malinda. She picked up some very interesting information as payment from Remi."

"And she's going to give us this information out of the kindness of her heart?" Helena asked the question before he could.

"I saved her life years ago, even before I formed the Circle of Sorcery. Whenever she learns something interesting, she sends it along, no charge. Malinda's been a good friend, make sure you show her the proper respect."

"I always show ladies the proper respect." Daisuke stood and grinned. "As long as they're not trying to kill me. Wish us luck, boss."

"I do. Take care, both of you. As soon as the matter is settled, let me know."

Daisuke nodded. "Will do, boss."

He helped Helena to her feet and they headed for the door. It was time to resume the search.

Daisuke and Helena landed two blocks from the warehouse where, they assumed, Remi and Vanessa had their battle. The trip through the shadow paths to Tamaz and the subsequent flight south had taken a little less than an hour. Even though she couldn't fly on her own, Helena did manage the invisibility barrier which saved him a fair bit of energy.

When they hit the ground, she blew out a breath and released the barrier. "I don't think I've ever maintained a spell for that long and I'm not eager to do so again. Where are we?"

"The manufacturing district a couple blocks from the target," Daisuke said. "I wanted to approach on foot to reduce the odds of a police wizard noticing us."

"You think there'll be one on site?"

"No idea, but better safe than sorry. Are you going to be okay with your personal invisibility spell? We can rest for a while if you need to. The warehouse isn't going anywhere."

"I'm fine and we don't have time to mess around."

Daisuke wasn't foolish enough to argue with her. "Okay. Ruq, fly ahead and see what we're dealing with."

He sensed the imp getting further away then, *Only two policemen, plain clothes. No wizards. You should be good to approach.*

"We're clear, let's go."

Daisuke turned invisible and a moment later Helena did as well. While he could still see the outline of her magical aura, to a non-wizard they would be undetectable. There were ways to hide from a wizard's magical vision as well, but that took a lot more time and effort.

The walk didn't take long though the smell of diesel fumes made it a good deal less than enjoyable. The front of the target warehouse had been blown to smithereens. Two people in tan jackets and holding notepads stood a few yards away. Those had to be the detectives. He'd expected to find a forensic team as well, but maybe they finished their work yesterday. That was good for Daisuke and Helena so he wasn't about to complain.

They snuck past the detectives and slipped into the building. Daisuke's boots crunched on the broken glass and debris strewn across the warehouse floor. He winced at the noise, but nothing from outside indicated they'd been detected. The scent of charred wood and scorched flesh lingered in the air while bloodstains dotted the floor, remnants of a vicious magical battle. Vanessa clearly hadn't held back.

They made a silent tour of the space and found nothing to indicate where either Vanessa or Remi had gone. The only thing of interest was the door-sized rectangle sliced in the back wall. He assumed someone, likely Remi, made his own emergency escape hatch.

Interesting as it was to view the site of the battle firsthand, it didn't net them much. Daisuke strode toward the front of the warehouse, Helena at his side. He had no idea where to search next. Bucharest was a big city after all. Maybe the boss's friend the information broker would have some intel for them.

He stopped by the door when a crackle sounded from the cops' radios. "Emergency! Officers down. Criminal wizard active in sector three. Send backup soonest."

"Should we go?" one of the cops asked his partner.

"No, we'd only be in the way. Let SWAT handle it. Our job is here."

The first man snorted. "We've found all there is to find. It's on forensics now and they won't be done for weeks."

The wizard had to be Vanessa. The problem was, sticking their noses into a fight between her and the police was likely to end up with more people getting hurt. But maybe they could track her from the air and strike when she reached a safe area.

He was about to suggest they do so when the rumble of an approaching motorcycle caught his attention. It was getting closer by the moment. The question was, why would a biker be coming here? If it was a criminal, he'd know enough to stay away from an active crime scene. And if it wasn't then coming here made even less sense.

Can you see them, Ruq?

Yes, Master. There's a big human in the front and a smaller one in the back. They'll be visible to you in a moment.

Sure enough a big black chopper came around the corner and drove right up beside the police car. Daisuke couldn't get a good look at the smaller man since he had his hood up, but he had a bad feeling.

"Hey!" one of the detectives said. "You can't be here, the area is restricted."

The smaller man got off the bike and pushed his hood back. It was Remi.

The two detectives headed toward the wizard, clearly clueless about what they were dealing with. He hesitated just long enough for Remi's magic to lash out and bind the detectives in place.

The motorcycle engine cut off and Remi looked right at Daisuke and Helena. "I know you're there. Show yourselves or these two die."

With innocent lives at risk, there was only one thing they could do. Daisuke and Helena released their invisibility spells.

"Remi," Daisuke said. "How unpleasant to see you again. What do you want?"

"Your help." Daisuke would've laughed if the situation were less serious. "Vanessa's on my trail and I can't shake her. I also can't beat her in a fight. But the three of us will make short work of her. You hate the Blood as much as I do. It's a win-win."

He had a point. Daisuke wouldn't feel bad about killing Vanessa. She was a psycho and the world would be better off without her in it. "Deal. But you have to let the police go first."

Remi snorted. "I don't think so. These two will ensure you don't turn on me as soon as we're done with Vanessa. My new minion will stay with them. As soon as Vanessa is dead and I'm a safe distance away, he'll let them go."

"And I'm supposed to trust you?" Daisuke asked.

Remi shrugged. "Do you have another option? I assume you don't want these two's deaths on your conscience."

He was right, damn the man. Daisuke couldn't let the cops die. Fortunately he did have another option.

"Fine, have it your way. Do you at least have a plan?"

"Sure. Like I said, she's got some way to track me. All I have to do is let her find me then we all attack at once. She'll be overwhelmed and dead in seconds."

Daisuke wasn't sure that counted as an actual plan, but it might work all the same.

"We can't do it here. It'll be too obvious you're planning something. There's a construction site down the road," Daisuke said. "We flew over it on the way here. It looked deserted. Should be perfect."

Remi nodded. "Sounds ideal. Lead the way."

Daisuke did so, Helena tense beside him. As they walked,

Daisuke reached out to Ruq. *Take out the biker at my signal. We have to time this just right.*

They'll still be enchanted, Master.

As long as they're not dead, I can deal with whatever magic Remi cast after the battle.

They reached the construction site soon enough. The half-built skeleton of a new warehouse towered behind a chain link fence. Cranes and other construction equipment sat here and there on the sides. Daisuke sensed nothing living within a block of the place. If there was going to be a fight, this was a good place for it. Hopefully whoever owned the warehouse had insurance.

"So what now?" Helena asked.

"Simple." Remi reached under his jacket, took out a shield amulet, and tossed it aside. "She'll have no trouble finding me now. You two had better hide. And remember, if you try anything the cops are dead."

As if Daisuke could forget what was at stake.

CHAPTER FOURTEEN

V anessa stood beside the flaming wreckage of the first cop car she blew up. Why the idiots had thought shooting at her would accomplish anything she couldn't begin to imagine. Normal people should be taught that wizards are, for the most part, bulletproof, unless you catch them by surprise. Not that those two would ever be taught anything again.

And now she was surrounded by the fools and Remi was long gone.

The crack of gunfire was giving her a headache. Cops swarmed from every direction, their faces twisted in fear and determination as they closed in on her.

A wave of her hand sent blue threads of flames lashing out in every direction.

Bulletproof vests proved considerably less proof against magic.

The number of pests was instantly reduced by a third.

"Pathetic." Vanessa wasn't even sure why she was wasting

her time with these cretins. She needed to catch up to Remi before he got any further away.

Her conjured barrier flared every time a bullet pinged off it, making it look like she was surrounded by fireflies. It was kind of pretty in a way, but she was growing tired of this game. It was time to finish it.

She threw her arms above her head. Power blazed around her as a wall of fire exploded skyward, cutting off the advancing police force. A whispered spell activated flight magic that shot her straight up into the air, leaving the chaos behind her as she soared away from the battlefield.

The nuisances should know better than to try and follow her. Pointless killing did nothing to advance her mission.

Vanessa's boots hit the ground in the middle of the parking lot of Remi's motel, sending a cloud of dust swirling around her. The smoke from her battle was visible in the distance and she could just smell the scorched asphalt and burnt rubber. She stalked toward her car, her thoughts already shifting to tracking Remi down.

She reached the parking lot and frowned. Her once-pristine car sat up on blocks, its tires stolen in the few minutes she'd been away.

"This day just keeps getting worse."

Shaking off her annoyance, Vanessa glanced around. A variety of junkers cluttered the motel parking lot. While not her preference, this wasn't the moment to be fussy.

She strode over, sizing up each vehicle until she found the least offensive option: a battered pickup truck that had seen better days. It was older than she was, but it would have to do. Assuming she could start the rust bucket.

A wave of her hand unlocked the door and she climbed inside. A second wave coaxed the engine to sputtering life. It roared when she touched the gas. That was a good sign. As long as it didn't quit halfway to wherever she was going next, she should be set.

Speaking of, Vanessa turned her attention to the compass. Remi couldn't have gotten far. She fed the compass a small amount of ether, and to her surprise, it immediately spun to life, the needle quivering as it pointed toward the warehouse district.

What was Remi playing at now? The shield amulet wouldn't have just stopped working, and Remi wasn't stupid enough to take it off by accident. It had to be a trap. She hadn't the least idea what the son of a bitch was planning and she didn't care. If he wanted a fight, she'd be happy to give it to him.

Gripping the steering wheel, she shifted the old truck into gear. It lurched then smoothed out and she was on her way.

Vanessa navigated the stolen truck through the city streets, every once in a while confirming that she was still on the right track. The arrow never wavered from the warehouse district. Why he would go back there she hadn't the least idea. Maybe he hoped to find more useless cops to send against her. They wouldn't take long to deal with.

She pulled up to a construction site, the skeletal structure of an unfinished warehouse towering over the truck. Remi stood there waiting for her, arms crossed, and looking as relaxed as could be. Maybe he wanted to die.

If that was the case, Vanessa would be happy to grant his wish, right after she tortured the location of Razak's prison out of him.

"Finally tired of running?" She climbed out of the truck and stalked toward him, fire gathering around her hands.

"Tell me where the demon prison is and I'll kill you quickly."

"Always so arrogant, Vanessa. Did you think I'd face you alone?"

Daisuke Kugo and Helena stepped out from behind a stack of construction material, their faces grim. Vanessa's gaze darted between them and Remi, her calculations about her chances of victory taking a rapid nosedive.

"Three against one hardly seems fair." She forced a laugh even as a cold sweat formed on her brow. "Why don't we make a deal? We can force Remi to tell us where the prison is, kill him, then work together to take out the Devil Man. Once we have the prison, we can decide between us who gets to keep it."

"Sorry, Vanessa." Daisuke's voice was cold as ice.

She turned to Helena but found no help there. Well, it wasn't a surprise. Had the circumstances been reversed and she had them outnumbered, mercy wouldn't have been offered either. What she couldn't figure out was why they were taking Remi's side.

She glared at the traitor, who stood there smirking, before shifting her gaze back to Daisuke and Helena. She knew she was outmatched, but there was no chance of retreat, not from these three.

"So be it, but I t go down easy."

Daisuke, Helena, and Remi faced Vanessa. There was tension in the air as each waited for the other to make the first move. In a wizard's duel, that first move could be your last. Daisuke gathered ether around him, readying it for easy casting. He'd never seen Vanessa in action, but she was of the blood, which guaranteed that she was stronger than the average wizard.

She was also every bit as impatient as he expected. Flames burst to life around her hands and a moment later she sent threads of blue flame streaking in at him.

Helena raised a golden barrier which slowed the threads a fraction before they cut through it. That gave Daisuke a fair idea of how strong Vanessa was. She was going to be a problem, but not an insurmountable one.

He rolled under the threads and pointed at her. Black lightning arced out, hitting Vanessa's personal shield and sending her skidding back.

As she forced herself to her feet, Remi decided to join in. Maybe he was hoping to strike the fatal blow. Daisuke had no idea and didn't care. He was distracted and that was the important thing.

Now, Ruq.

Trusting his familiar to handle a single human, Daisuke hit Vanessa with another lightning blast. This time she was blown back into her truck with rib-cracking force. She slid down, her beautiful face twisted in pain.

Remi closed in, confirming Daisuke's theory that he wanted to finish his former comrade off personally. Daisuke edged closer as well. Killing Vanessa would no doubt improve the world a great deal, but she was a side matter. Remi was his focus today.

Three strides from Vanessa, Remi stumbled, his face twisted in pain.

Got him, Master.

Daisuke didn't hesitate.

He lunged forward, grabbed Remi's head, and pumped it full of black lightning.

Remi's body twitched and spasmed as the spell burned the life out of him. When there was nothing left, he lowered Remi's body to the ground.

He didn't have long now. A cocoon of ether formed around Remi's body. Focusing with all he had, Daisuke sought and found the ghostly form of Remi's soul as it tried to escape and make its way to its final destination, likely Abaddon's hell.

He wasn't going to get away so easily. Activating one of his darker arts, Daisuke stitched soul to body with ethereal thread. Not in any way that would allow Remi to function, just enough to make sure he wouldn't be able to refuse the compulsion spells Daisuke planned to use later.

"She's escaping!" Helena said.

He barely heard her, so total was his focus. Stitching a soul to a body was no easy feat.

When it was done he looked up and found Helena scowling down at him. Somehow she made even that expression look beautiful.

"What did you say?" he asked.

"I said, she's getting away. Though now I need to amend that to, she got away. I tried to stop her, but she blew through my bindings like they were nothing and flew off." Helena made a disgusted gesture to the east. "What are you doing anyway?"

"I bound Remi's soul to his body. Now I can make him tell us everything, including how to find Razak's prison. Much as I would've liked to finish off Vanessa, I had to act when he was distracted by Ruq killing his minion."

She made a face. Sometimes people forgot Daisuke's first

and primary magical profession was necromancer. This was the sort of thing he trained for.

"And Vanessa?" Helena asked.

"She's a problem for another day. A day I'm sure will come far sooner than we might like. I need to make a quick trip, will you be okay here on your own for a few minutes?"

"Sure. I'll go see what I can do about the detectives. Where are you going?"

"To one of my bolt-holes. It's not a nice place, but it is good for what I need to do with Remi. I'd take you with me, but I can only carry one body."

Ruq landed on his shoulder. A gesture levitated Remi's corpse high enough for Daisuke to grab it. That done, he stepped through the nearest shadow.

A moment later he emerged in a clearing surrounded by tall, ancient oak trees. There was nothing living in the circle. The ground was devoid of life and had been for a very long time. Something horrible had happened here in a distant war and the earth was cursed and corrupted. Normal people instinctively avoided this place which made it perfect for a necromancer like Daisuke.

"I've never been here before," Ruq said. "It kind of gives me Castle Ravenclaw vibes."

"This is a different sort of corruption, but you're not far wrong. The corrupt aura makes it a good place for casting darker spells. The nature of the ether here enhances them. I found this place before I found you and I've never had a reason to come back. Now I do."

He dumped Remi's body on the ground and pointed. The corrupted earth swallowed him up.

"Good. When we get back tonight he should be saturated and ready for questioning."

"You know," Ruq said. "If you wanted to create powerful undead, this would be the perfect place for it."

"Are you trying to corrupt my soul? You haven't tried that since I first made a pact with you."

"I'm an imp; it's part of the job."

Daisuke grinned. "I'm pleased to say you're not very good at it. Though if anyone asks, I'll be sure and tell them you did your best."

"I appreciate that, Master."

They shadow walked back to the warehouse and emerged in time to see Helena picking away at the spells that held the detectives bound. He hadn't paid much attention earlier but it turned out one was a woman and the other a man. Neither of them had been harmed, though their bodies were still rigid.

"Finish your mystery errand?" Helena asked without looking away from her work.

"Yup. Once the sun sets, I'll be ready to ask my questions." That wasn't all he planned to do, but no sense talking about it when they had extra ears around. "Need a hand?"

"Sure, take the other one."

Daisuke went to the man and offered his most reassuring smile. "I'll have you free in no time. Don't worry, we're the good guys."

A few ethereal snips and slices and the detective staggered around like a drunk.

"Easy," Daisuke said. "It'll take your body a few minutes to regain full mobility. Sitting might be a good idea until then."

The detective fell on his butt more than sat, but at least he was safely down. "Thanks. Who the hell are you people?"

"The good guys, like I said. My partner and I travel the world dealing with rogue wizards like Remi. That's the guy who paralyzed you. He's dead by the way, so you should be all set."

"You know what happened at the warehouse?" the detective asked.

"I don't know the details beyond the fact that two wizards got into a fight and a bunch of drug-dealing scumbags got killed in the crossfire. A good result if you ask me."

"Personally, I agree, but the captain expects a bit more in my report. Your name for starters."

Daisuke grinned, stood, and moved aside so Helena could guide the second officer down beside her partner. "Sorry, that's need to know and you don't need to know. Good luck to you, Detective."

He took Helena's hand and led her into the warehouse. From there it was a short shadow walk back to the construction site.

"Why are we here?" Helena asked.

"We still need to visit the magic district and collect the boss's intel, remember?"

From her expression, Daisuke was pretty sure she did not, in fact, remember. Hardly a surprise given everything that had happened. But it shouldn't take long to pick up what they needed and return home.

Once they made their report and the sun set, Daisuke would see what Remi's useless soul had to say for itself.

CHAPTER FIFTEEN

Daisuke knocked on the boss's office door. He and Helena had just gotten back from Bucharest and he was anxious to debrief so he could start making preparations for the ritual tonight. The door swung open and the boss shifted her gaze to the sheaf of papers in Daisuke's hand.

"Malinda's report?" she asked.

"Yup. I don't know where you found her, but she's a character. Her assessments of Remi and Vanessa were spot on. Speaking of those two, Remi's dead but Vanessa got away. Technically I let her get away, but it was unavoidable."

"Come in and tell me everything." The boss took the papers from him but didn't look at them.

When they had all settled into their usual seats, Daisuke got started. He left nothing out and when he finished said, "It's a shame Vanessa escaped since I doubt she'll just give up."

"You're not wrong," the boss said. "But done is done. I admit the soul binding makes me a bit uncomfortable. Heaven's law states we're not to meddle with mortal souls unless absolutely necessary. Doing so puts your own soul in danger of being corrupted."

Helena shot him a quick, worried look, but didn't comment. He appreciated her concern and her willingness not to talk about it. Daisuke had long since made peace with his decisions.

He shrugged. "I did what I had to if we want to find Razak's prison. Besides, I've already got a demon familiar. I'm sure that did more to corrupt my soul than performing a little necromancy on a piece of shit like Remi."

Hey!

Daisuke didn't let his amusement at Ruq's comment show. He also bit back the urge to mention his plan included more than just questioning Remi. Some things were better left unsaid.

"I guess a fallen angel isn't the best person to be giving a lecture on Heaven's laws." The boss's voice held a hint of self-deprecation mingled with reluctant acceptance. "Just be sure to take care of yourself."

"I will." Daisuke had been taking care of himself for a long time. He wasn't about to stop now. He also wasn't going to let a bunch of arrogant assholes get away with screwing up the world because they thought they were entitled to power, or control, or whatever other stupid, useless thing they wanted.

"What's so important about those papers?" Helena asked, breaking some of the grim mood.

"You didn't look at them?" the boss asked, her golden eyes shimmering with restrained excitement. "Remi traded Malinda the names and abilities of every member of the Blood of Solomon for his shield amulet."

Daisuke's eyebrows rose and he let out a low whistle. "Nice for us. Of course, I'd be surprised if he knew everything there was to know about the group."

"True." The boss couldn't stop her gaze from shifting back to the documents. "But it's more information than we had before. Every little advantage helps. I'll have Crystal type these up and send a copy out to all our agents."

"Good plan." He stood and stretched. "I have some work to finish before tonight. Questioning a soul isn't the sort of thing you want to do half prepared."

"Can I help?" Helena asked, her concern plain in both her expression and tone.

Daisuke shook his head. "Thanks, but no. This is something best done on my own."

"If you're sure, but please don't do anything too crazy."

"You know me." He offered a half-hearted grin.

"Yes," Helena said, not buying his act for a second. "That's why I'm worried."

Daisuke wasn't sure what to say, so he said nothing. What he was going to do had to happen, so it would. If it damaged his soul, then so be it. Hopefully the good of sealing away Razak's prison would balance the scales.

＊

Vanessa blasted through the air as fast as her meager remaining magic could propel her. Near-death experiences seemed to be her new lot in life. First the dungeon of Castle Ravenclaw, then the battle with Daisuke, Helena, and Remi. Those three fighting together wasn't something she expected to happen. Maybe it was an "enemy of my enemy is my friend" sort of situation. Though Vanessa considered herself less reprehensible than Remi, she couldn't say what two Circle agents might think.

Though given the speed with which Daisuke turned on Remi, it was possible Vanessa was reading the situation incorrectly. One thing was certain: Remi was now very dead and her best hope of finding Razak's prison died with him.

But that was far from her most pressing concern. Her whole body ached and felt weak. The black lightning had drained a fair bit of her strength despite her magical barrier. She needed to get back to headquarters and alert Lord Solomon to what had happened. Having to report another failure left a bitter taste in her mouth, but given the alternative, she wasn't about to complain.

Vanessa landed outside her hotel and pushed through the revolving door. Staff members attired in crisp uniforms stared as she passed. She paid them not the least attention as she hurried to the elevators. A quick ride up brought her to the peace and quiet of her room. Vanessa caught a glimpse of her reflection in a mirror and paused. No wonder the help was staring at her. Her clothes were torn, her face bruised, and the ends of a couple strands of hair still smoldered.

To call her a mess would be generous.

She shook it all off and threw her few belongings in her satchel. Only one item remained out, a ten-inch stick engraved with runes. The teleportation stick was her ticket back to Castle Solomon. She ran her finger along the length, feeling the bump of the runes. Lord Solomon's words of caution about Daisuke's strength had been an understatement. Vanessa hadn't wanted to believe them, her pride wouldn't allow it, but now she couldn't deny the truth. He really was as close to Lord Solomon's equal as there was in the world.

Just thinking about it terrified her.

With a sigh, Vanessa snapped the stick. An instant later she stood in the teleportation chamber of the castle. She took a moment to revel in the feeling of safety the sandstone walls always brought her. There was nowhere else in the world she could call home.

The hall beyond the chamber was empty. No apprentice had come to guide her to the meeting hall. Since it was impossible Lord Solomon didn't know she'd returned, she had to assume he was busy with something else at the moment. That suited her fine. A little time to clean up and decompress would be welcome.

She marched down the empty passages to her quarters. They were nothing special, just a bedroom and bathroom with minimal furniture. Her satchel went on the floor, the compass she tossed on the bed before stripping off her charred garments. A hot shower washed the soot from her skin. Pity it did nothing to restore her strength, but that would be asking a lot from water. Clean and dry, she put on a new red blouse and dark trousers before heading out again.

Vanessa made her way through the silent halls to the meeting room. She couldn't help wondering why she hadn't been summoned. Surely Lord Solomon didn't doubt her value to the group.

No, Vanessa couldn't think that way. He was probably busy. It wasn't like he spent all his time sitting around waiting to hear from her. No matter how big of an ego she might have, it couldn't be that large.

Outside the door to the meeting room, she paused to gather her resolve and steady her shaken nerves. When she was ready, she knocked.

"Enter," Lord Solomon said.

Pushing the door open, Vanessa stepped into the room. At the head of the table Solomon the Great sat alone, his white hair and beard and his tan robe perfect as always. Looking at him made her ashamed of how she'd arrived not so long ago.

"Vanessa," he said, the single word so full of kindness and compassion that all her worries faded away.

"Lord Solomon, I regret to say that I've failed again."

"Sit and tell me all about it."

Vanessa did as he bid and soon the story came pouring out of her. She made no effort to lessen her failure. There was no point. She finished by saying, "I apologize for my failure. With Remi dead, there's no way to recover Razak's prison."

"What makes you so certain?" he asked.

"I don't understand," Vanessa said. "Who else can guide us to it?"

"Do you imagine Daisuke isn't going to go and claim the prison? He's a necromancer. A dead prisoner is no obstacle for him. You have the compass?"

"Of course, my lord." She handed it over.

"I need to recalibrate it to point to Daisuke rather than Remi. He is of the blood and so can be found just as easily. You will follow him and claim the prison."

Vanessa couldn't believe she was about to say this. "He's too strong for me. He proved that in Bucharest."

"For you alone, certainly, however, you shall not be alone. One of our brothers has returned from a mission just this day." He turned his gaze toward the chamber door. "Come in, Haakon."

The door swung open and in strode Haakon Lybeck, looking like a Viking from the Norse sagas, a towering figure of muscle, his blond hair long and flowing behind him. Erik's Helm, the source of Haakon's greatest power, was tucked under his arm. While far from Vanessa's favorite member of the group, she would be glad to have him at her side in a fight.

"Haakon." Vanessa offered a polite nod.

"Vanessa." Haakon's voice dripped contempt. "You failed again."

She bristled but before she could snap back Lord Solomon said, "You lost to Daisuke as well, Haakon. Don't be so quick to judge your sister."

Haakon flinched at the words. "Forgive me, Master."

"Did you find the prison you were sent to claim?" Vanessa asked.

"There was no prison, just a wild demon that I cut down. Hardly even a challenge."

"The two of you will travel to Castle Ravenclaw," Lord Solomon said. "The corruption will hide your presence. When Daisuke arrives in the area, follow him to the cult's hidden base and claim Razak's prison."

"And kill Daisuke?" Haakon asked as much as stated.

"If possible, that would be ideal. We need to claim the staff at some point. But the prison is your priority. If the boy lives another day, it would be an annoyance, but nothing more."

Vanessa had no desire to return to Castle Ravenclaw—too many bad memories—but if that's what it took to redeem herself, then she would do so. No matter what, Vanessa refused to return a three-time failure.

CHAPTER SIXTEEN

Daisuke appeared in his apartment and grimaced at the mess. His kitchen table was covered with the books and scrolls he'd taken from Remi's workshop in Castle Ravenclaw. He hoped to find some new spells, assuming he ever got the time to read them.

"Weren't you supposed to put this stuff in the vault along with the artifacts we found?" Ruq asked.

"Technically. The Circle can have them once I'm finished. I consider it my bonus for years of hard work." Daisuke put the books out of his mind. They were a treat for later.

He went to his bedroom, stopped in front of a blank section of wall, and traced an intricate symbol in the air. A glowing ethereal rune appeared and seared itself into the wall. A three-foot-square section shimmered and vanished, revealing an invisible storage area. Rows of specialized tools gleamed in his magical sight.

Daisuke gathered what he needed—a silver dagger, an obsidian bowl, and a red crystal—and placed them in his satchel. Lastly he tossed his gloves and phone on the bed. He needed maximum control for this ritual and anything that reduced his feel for the ether had to go.

"Okay, let's do this."

Another trip through the shadow paths brought them back to the corrupted grove. The spot where he buried Remi's body remained undisturbed, exactly as he'd expected. His expectations aside, when dealing with a ritual, it was always good to confirm everything. Some newly minted wizards failed to realize how even the tiniest thing could screw up a complex ritual. He wanted to do this right the first time.

Judging by the length of the shadows, he had about six hours until sunset. That should be plenty of time to forge the talisman.

Daisuke's boots crunched on the dead earth as he approached the edge of the grove. The air held a hint of decay. He scanned the surrounding trees until he spotted the one he wanted, an ancient dead oak. From the size of it, the tree had probably been here longer than the corruption. Perfect, it should've soaked up plenty of negative energy.

An ethereal blade appeared at his mental command and sliced a six-inch length of branch off. That should be plenty for what he needed. Two more slices squared up the ends.

"I don't think I've seen you do proper necromancy," Ruq said.

"It's seldom necessary given my day-to-day work. Anti-spirit magic is a branch of necromancy and much more useful for fighting demons than this sort of thing. Creating powerful undead, while potentially valuable, wouldn't go over well with my coworkers, much less the boss."

"No, I suppose even a fallen angel would frown on the creation of undead." Ruq grinned. "Though if she knew what you had planned for tonight, I don't think she'd approve either."

Daisuke shrugged. He had great respect for the boss and everyone else in the Circle, but their squeamishness could be a problem sometimes. He didn't use the darker skills he'd learned lightly, but when you were trying to protect the world, you couldn't let your morals stand in the way of completing the mission.

"Keep quiet now. I need to concentrate." Branch in hand, Daisuke returned to the center of the clearing.

He knelt on the barren ground, laying out his tools with the precision of a surgeon. The silver dagger flashed in the sunlight. It looked almost too pure for this sort of work, but that purity served an important balance to the darkness. The obsidian bowl, on the other hand, served the opposite function. It would gather and enhance the corruption, making the spell more effective. Finally, he produced the red crystal that would serve as the heart of the talisman.

Each had its purpose and it was up to Daisuke to meld them into a single, cohesive unit.

With a practiced hand, Daisuke lifted the silver dagger and began to inscribe a series of intricate runes onto the dead branch. Each rune blazed with black flames when it formed. Last he carved out an indentation in the end of the stick. The silver did its job, protecting his hands from the corruption. When the task was completed, the once-razor-sharp edge was dull as a butter knife and he knew without question he would never be able to use the blade again. Pity, given how expensive silver daggers were.

Now for stage two. He placed the stick over the obsidian bowl and bathed it in concentrated corruption. The dead wood soaked it up like a sponge. As he hoped, years of exposure to the site's ambient energy had made the wood a perfect vessel.

Using tongs made of ether, Daisuke placed the red crystal in the indentation he'd made at the tip of the stick. Guiding the magic, he molded the wood like clay, locking the crystal in place.

When the wood could hold no more corruption, Daisuke ended the spell. The talisman was complete.

"Let's hope Remi's soul is ready for its interview," Ruq said, his voice somewhat gleeful. It seemed doing something that felt evil had put the imp in a good mood.

"Ready or not," Daisuke said. "He's going to answer my questions."

Daisuke returned his tools to his satchel and cleared his mind. The coming confrontation wouldn't be easy or pleasant. Souls experienced pain differently than living flesh, so if Remi forced him to compel the answers he needed, it would be tricky, but Daisuke wouldn't hesitate to do what he had to.

When the sun had set, Daisuke moved to stand in front of Remi's makeshift grave. He extended his hand, palm upturned, and a simple motion beckoned forth Remi's corpse. A spectral force exhumed the body, raising it into the air where it hovered, motionless, like a puppet without a puppeteer.

He turned his attention to the talisman, guiding it over to float a foot away from the cadaver. Another intricate gesture conjured a spell circle beneath them. Preparations complete, Daisuke yanked Remi's soul out of his body. The ghostly form howled and raged with incoherent, beast-like wails. Had anyone been in the area, those cries would give them nightmares for the rest of their life.

Daisuke blocked them out and focused. He had enough nightmare fuel; a little more made no difference to him. Inch by inch he forced Remi's soul into the talisman. It fought hard, not wanting to be separated from its proper vessel.

The spell circle thrummed when the fusion of talisman and spirit was complete.

He blew out a breath and released the magic. That had been every bit as unpleasant as he'd expected. You didn't mess with these sorts of powers and expect to get out of it scot-free.

But the worst of it was done now. Remi's soul was bound and at his mercy. It was time to see what the son of a bitch had to say for himself.

He snatched the talisman out of the air and sent a psychic call. Remi's ghostly head emerged from the crystal.

"Please, Daisuke! Don't do this. I beg you to set me free." Remi's spectral voice held true dread as he spoke.

"I may, assuming you make yourself useful. Should you do otherwise, I swear this talisman will be your soul's final resting place. Speaking of resting places..."

Daisuke snapped his fingers and Remi's body crumbled to dust. With the trash taken care of he returned his focus to Remi. "What did you and the Devil Man have planned for Razak?"

"Our plan?" Remi said. "No, I had my plan and he had his. The Devil Man wants to merge with Razak, claiming the elder demon's power for himself. I told him I could make that happen. And I can, sort of. The process is similar to how I made Vixen only on a greater scale. The results would've been the same as well, a powerful new servant under my control. It seems my dream will never come to pass now."

"And thank heaven for that," Daisuke said. "Can you lead us to the cult's hidden temple?"

"I can. There's a trick to finding your way through the barrier. But even if you do it right, the Devil Man will sense your arrival."

Daisuke shrugged. "I didn't think we'd be able to sneak up on him in his own temple. Does he have anywhere else he can run to?"

"Not that I know of."

"Good." Exhaustion was building along with the first hint of a backlash headache. With a final gesture, he banished Remi's soul into the silent depths of the talisman.

He'd learned what he needed to. Tomorrow, he'd deal with the Devil Man once and for all.

CHAPTER SEVENTEEN

"If we never have to come back here, I'd be okay with that," Helena said.

Daisuke couldn't argue. He'd been spending far too much time in and around Castle Ravenclaw for his liking. Right now they were back where the hunt began, right outside the trapped exit of the emergency escape tunnel. He meant to start at the beginning and make damn sure they didn't miss anything. Razak's prison was around here somewhere and Daisuke didn't plan to leave until he found it. If he could kill the Devil Man in the process, so much the better.

His fingers tightened around the blackened wood of the soul talisman. The runes sparked with black lightning, but they didn't cause him any discomfort. He'd dealt with far greater quantities of corruption over the past few years to let such a tiny amount phase him.

"Okay, Remi, you're up." Focusing his will, he compelled Remi's ghostly head to appear.

"You bound him?" Helena asked or, more accurately,

accused. "You said you were only going to question Remi's soul, not take it prisoner."

"I didn't say I wasn't going to bind his soul. We need to find the temple and this is the surest way to do so. Once things are settled, I can set him free. I suspect whatever hell claims him will treat him worse."

She still looked pissed, but at least no more complaints were forthcoming. That was just as well. Daisuke liked Helena a lot, but she had a soft streak a mile wide. It was an endearing trait, but also a liability when hard things needed to be done.

"Remi." He turned his full focus on the prisoner. "You will lead us to the temple. You will take a safe path and warn us of any traps."

"There are no safe paths. There is only one path and if you choose to walk it, the Devil Man will know as soon as you arrive. Not that he can do much about it given our meager resources. Turn forty-five degrees to the right of the false path. You'll find a line of spruce trees running basically straight north. Follow them until you see the stone marker. Once you reach the marker, you only need to find the entrance. It's between two black oaks."

Sounded simple enough as long as you knew the way. Daisuke took the lead, trying his best to estimate the angle of travel. He must've done something right as about a hundred yards from the tunnel he spotted the first spruce.

"I'm surprised he told us the truth," Helena said.

"Why? Even if Remi wanted to lie to me, and I'm sure he did, the binding magic doesn't allow it. He has to do exactly what I tell him. Should he do otherwise, the magic will punish him. Souls can feel pain, you know. Disembodied souls I mean. Most people think they're invincible, but if you know the right magic, nothing is invincible."

"I'm not sure knowing how to hurt a soul is something you should be boasting about."

"I'm not boasting, I'm explaining how I know we can trust Remi's word."

The conversation trailed off and Daisuke was fine with the quiet. He had no interest in explaining himself to anyone, including Helena. He did what he had to and that was the end of it. If someone had a problem with the decisions he made, that was on them, not him.

They followed the line of spruces for he wasn't sure how long before he spotted a square stone beside the trail. No stone like that ever existed in nature. It had to be the marker.

"Is this it?" Daisuke asked.

"Yes," Remi said. "The black oaks are a little further."

Ten strides on, he spotted them. The oaks weren't that big, but they stood out among the evergreens like a duck among seagulls. The space between them was only big enough for them to pass through single file. He sent Remi back into the talisman and tucked it away in his satchel. Before they passed through the entrance, he summoned his trunk and took out the Staff of Law. While he felt confident the prison couldn't be opened without the seal, he wanted to be ready on the off chance he was wrong.

He glanced at Helena. "You ready?"

"As I'll ever be."

Hand in hand they stepped one after the other through the gap between the trunks.

It was a bit anticlimactic. On the other side was nothing but more forest and a stone path that ran to a passage dug into the ground. Going from living in a castle to living in a hole in the ground was a considerable downgrade. No doubt the Devil Man's ego didn't like that. The thought pleased Daisuke no end.

"Other than an increase in the ambient corruption, I don't sense anything," Helena said.

"Neither do I." Daisuke let go of her hand to free himself up to fight. "What say we take a closer look?"

Together, they marched toward the hole. At the bottom was a black iron door attached to a stone frame. Daisuke poked it open with the staff, revealing a dark stone passage. It had to have been created with magic. There was nothing around here save soft dirt. There were no obvious traps visible to either his magical or mundane vision. With a shrug he stepped forward into the tunnel.

Nothing happened.

"You want to handle the light?"

Helena had a hand over her mouth and looked on the verge of throwing up.

"Yeah, the corruption is pretty thick down here. It's not as bad as the dungeon though. You should still be able to use your magic." He tried to sound encouraging but wasn't sure how well he managed.

"I hate places like this." She took her hand away from her mouth and gestured. A feeble golden light sprang to life. If that was the best she could manage, he was tempted to have her wait topside. Of course that had risks of its own.

"Want me to scout ahead?" Ruq asked.

"No, we stick together."

Ruq didn't argue and neither did Helena. Both of them were too smart for that.

They pressed onward, the only sound their footfalls on the stone. Daisuke couldn't sense anything through the background corruption. They were advancing blind. Far from ideal, but the only option at the moment.

"Where the hell is everyone?" Helena asked.

"Remi said they didn't have much in the way of resources. I'll bet they're waiting in the altar chamber for us to arrive. The Devil Man's magic will be strongest in the seat of Abaddon's worship. When we get there, leave him to me and take out any cultists you see. Ruq, if you spot the prison, grab it and take it somewhere safe."

"Safe? In a temple of Abaddon?" Ruq said.

"You know what I mean." He spotted a door up ahead and the talking stopped.

He used the staff to poke it open, ready to lash out at any threat. All he found was a bleak, unoccupied bedroom. If a hard bed, a footlocker, and a wash basin were the best rewards a cultist could expect, Daisuke didn't know how they recruited anyone.

They passed three more equally uninteresting rooms before coming face to face with a stone door carved with the flaming skull symbol of Abaddon. "I bet this is the place," Daisuke said.

"No kidding," Helena said. "What gave it away?"

He grinned. It was nice to see she'd gotten some of her spirit back.

The door pushed open on silent, well-oiled hinges. Beyond it waited a black stone altar draped with a red cloth sporting the same symbol as the door. The Devil Man stood behind the altar, three human cultists to his right and one of the smashed-face demons to his left. If this was all they had to deal with, the fight shouldn't be as bad as he'd feared.

What worried him was the absence of the prison. It had to be hidden around here somewhere. He shook his head.

They could look for it later. First the crazy demon worshipers had to go.

○

Vanessa hated Castle Ravenclaw. Nothing here but bad memories. When she escaped the last time, her dearest wish had been to never return. As usual, her wish wasn't granted. So here she stood, in these forsaken corridors foul with the stench of demonic corruption, waiting for the man who had nearly killed her to return. And if that wasn't bad enough, all she had for company was the growling, scowling Haakon Lybeck.

All in all, life could've been better.

She fed a little ether into the compass. It slowly reacted, turning west and a little north. He was still in Zurich, no doubt sleeping in his comfortable bed or enjoying a delicious meal or doing just about anything more pleasant than hunkering down in a former cult base.

"I weary of this," Haakon said. "How much longer are we going to have to wait?"

"I haven't the least idea. Daisuke wasn't kind enough to provide me with his itinerary." Vanessa looked up from the compass. "If it makes you feel better, I'm not enjoying myself either."

"It doesn't. Your failure is the reason we're here. You alone deserve to be miserable."

"The last I heard, you hadn't brought in a single prison or seal. And Daisuke about killed you the last time you ran into him, so spare me your self-righteousness."

"He caught me in a moment of weakness after a battle with Cristo. That will not happen a second time."

"Spare me your excuses as well. You failed. I failed. And that's the plain truth. This is our chance to make up for it. If that means we have to wait until doomsday, then so be it."

His only answer was a snarl. She didn't care as long as it was a silent snarl.

She sent ether into the compass again and this time the needle snapped almost due north. He was here, and close.

"Your wish has been granted. The compass says he's here."

"At last." Haakon pushed away from the wall and stuck Erik's Helm on his head. "Let's go kill him."

"Idiot. We follow him and claim the prison, remember? Those were Lord Solomon's orders. Killing Daisuke is a bonus, not the main job." She didn't move until Haakon gave her a reluctant nod of acceptance.

While she didn't trust Haakon not to lose his focus once they caught sight of Daisuke, for now it was enough. They had no time to delay.

They hurried out of the castle and worked their way slowly around the wall before turning north at the compass's urging. Vanessa grimaced as they entered the shadowy forest. She hated the wilderness. At least there were no bugs or thorn bushes.

"There's a faint trail," Haakon said. "He's making no effort at stealth."

"Why would he? It's not like he knows we're here." The compass needle remained rock steady and Vanessa trusted it way more than Haakon's tracking skills.

As if to mock her, ten paces later the compass's needle stopped responding. Even overloading it with ether produced no reaction. "Damn it, not again."

"What's the problem?" Haakon asked from behind her.

"The compass is dead. He must have passed through the cult's barrier."

"If that's true, we must be close. Step aside, I can follow their tracks."

Vanessa had no idea if he could do what he claimed or not, but she was out of ideas.

Haakon moved ahead of her, his eyes scanning the ground as he did a credible impression of a seasoned tracker.

The pace was painfully slow, but at last Haakon stopped. What was different about this miserable stretch of forest she had no idea. "What's the problem?"

"There's no problem. The tracks disappear here." Haakon nodded toward a couple of trees. "This must be the entrance to the barrier."

"Finally." She hesitated. It would be a problem if they crossed the barrier only to find Daisuke waiting on the other side for them. Should they wait a little longer?

Her internal debate ended when, without a word to her, Haakon crossed the threshold. Cursing the stupid, arrogant Vg, she followed.

The Devil Man lounged in his clandestine office. Since his less-than-encouraging conversation with Abaddon, he'd been spending all his time distracting himself from his problems. His preferred method of doing so was the hookah he kept in the corner of the office. The smoke he inhaled served no mystical purpose, it was just a pleasant intoxicant.

He'd heard nothing from Remi, hardly a surprise given

the brief time the man had been gone. It didn't help that the temple's isolation barrier ensured the only way to get an update was for him to return and make a direct report. That wouldn't happen for at least a week and probably longer.

No, all the Devil Man could do was wait. Wait for lesser beings to make his dreams come true. Was this how the demon lords felt when they were forced to deal with mere mortals? A sad thought if true.

He had the mouthpiece halfway to his lips when a subtle shift in the ether caught his attention. He recognized it at once; an intruder had passed through the barrier.

A surge of magic burned away his lethargy and the Devil Man expanded his awareness. Whoever they were, the two intruders were still aboveground and approaching slowly. Pity the magic didn't provide any details, but then again it was enough to know that anyone coming here uninvited was an enemy and therefore had to die.

The Devil Man pushed himself out of his chair. Given his meager defenses, dealing with powerful intruders would be a problem. But not an insurmountable one.

"Everyone meet me in the altar chamber at once!" he shouted, his magically enhanced voice reaching every cultist in the temple.

He strode into the altar chamber, pulling up his hood as he did so. An imposing figure already, he took on the aspect of something more than human. What he was about to do would require utter faith from his followers and to get that, you needed to project the right aura. The Devil Man excelled at the technique.

His three followers knelt in front of the altar as he approached. Beside them, a lesser hellfire demon waited for orders, its smashed-in face focusing on him despite the lack of eyes.

"Master," one of the cultists said. "What are your commands?"

"Enemies have breached the barrier and will be here soon. If there is to be any hope of defeating them, it will require a sacrifice. The three of you will be well rewarded by our master when you arrive in his hell."

The cultists exchanged nervous glances. It seemed they harbored doubts about the fate of their immortal souls. A bit late for such concerns, but when faced with imminent death, they were unavoidable.

"Have no fear. Lord Abaddon will recognize and honor your faith. You have been devout in your service and there can be no greater act than to sacrifice yourself for the cause." Magic wove through his words and when he finished their doubts were gone.

Excellent.

"Stand ready," the Devil Man said. "When the intruders enter we will show them the strength of your faith."

The cultists rested their hands on the ceremonial daggers at their belts. He sensed no more doubts.

When the door opened revealing the hated wizards who had ruined his bonding with Razak, the Devil Man snarled.

"Abaddon, accept this offering!" He threw his hands up and a hell portal opened behind him.

At his command, the cultists drew their daggers and drove them into their own chests. Life force rushed out of them and into the portal.

A deep, dark voice said, "Your service has ended."

The Devil Man's eyes widened in horror as the hand of

Abaddon ripped his soul out of his body along with his servants'. He howled at the burning agony even as he knew it was only the beginning of his suffering.

To fail a demon lord was to know endless agony.

CHAPTER EIGHTEEN

Daisuke's heart pounded as he watched the souls of Abaddon's followers get sucked into the hell portal. The cultists he could understand—they were useless in a fight—but why did the Devil Man sacrifice himself? It made no sense for a power-hungry megalomaniac to die willingly.

"We are in so much trouble," Daisuke muttered as the demon roared and convulsed. It kept expanding, muscles bulging grotesquely, sinews stretching as it grew larger, more formidable.

Daisuke hurled a bolt of black lightning, hoping to take it out before it got any bigger.

He might as well have spit on it for all the good the spell did. A barrier repelled his attack. It looked like it was powered by the hell portal, which meant there was nothing he could do but wait for the transformation to run its course.

"What the hell just happened?" Helena's voice trembled, not a surprising reaction to watching four people, even four deranged cultists, kill themselves.

"Abaddon claimed the Devil Man's soul," Ruq said. "Probably got sick of his constant screwups. Demon lords aren't known for their patience. At least Abaddon isn't. The cult was just about used up anyway. Their sacrifice opened the way for all the juicy power that's upgrading a low-tier claw demon into whatever that thing's going to be."

"Great, at least the Devil Man is out of the picture. I'll take my silver linings where I can find them." Daisuke observed the demon's expansion. It had turned into a hulking monstrosity of muscle and malice easily eight feet tall and flickering with hellfire. At least the process seemed to be slowing down.

"Helena, keep your distance," he said. "Focus on healing me. This is going to be rough. Ruq, stay high and watch my back. I'm pretty sure we're the only ones here, but if I'm wrong, I'd prefer to not get jumped from behind."

Helena, bless her heart, stayed silent. Daisuke had fought more demons than she'd seen, and experience counted in these situations.

"Don't get yourself killed," Ruq said. "If I lose my link to the mortal world in a temple of Abaddon, let's just say it wouldn't go well for me."

The imp turned invisible and flew up to the roof.

Daisuke nodded once, steeling himself against the surge of adrenaline that threatened to overwhelm his senses. He knew the fight ahead would test the limits of his abilities. But he was ready, as ready as any man could be when facing the fury of Hell.

The air crackled with tension. Daisuke leveled the staff in preparation for launching a spell as soon as the demon lost its aura of protection. And it wouldn't be long now. The demon was already a towering beast nearly half again

Daisuke's height. Hellfire ran along its body and pooled in its hands, ready to unleash. He put it at high tier five, maybe even tier six. That was pretty close to his limit for a one-on-one fight.

Its aura vanished and Daisuke hurled a bolt of black lightning. The spell struck it dead center in the chest and burned a little black spot that healed in an instant.

Okay, that wasn't the result he'd been hoping for.

The demon roared and sent a stream of hellfire rushing at him.

Daisuke dove and rolled to his feet, sending a counterblast of lightning into the demon's face. A jutting fang exploded into shards of bone.

That was a little better.

The demon surged forward and swung its clawed hand.

Daisuke leapt, kicked off its wrist, and landed on the opposite side. The swipe gouged four long stripes out of the stone floor, leaving them glowing orange, the stone partially melted.

He made a mental note to not let the claws hit him.

The battle raged around the chamber. Abaddon's altar was smashed to pieces by an errant swing. All of Daisuke's spells proved nearly or totally ineffective. He needed time to build his power into a single spell, but the demon had no intention of giving it to him.

Just as Daisuke prepared to unleash another futile bolt of lightning, the altar room's heavy doors burst open. Vanessa and Haakon strode into the chamber and looked around at the chaos.

Daisuke barely had time to register their arrival before Haakon charged him, his body surrounded by the golden glow of his magical armor, and a matching ax in his right hand.

Haakon made it halfway across the chamber before the demon noticed him.

A backhand swipe sent the man flying into the wall with bone-shattering force. He popped to his feet, unharmed, an instant later.

Forming a desperate plan, Daisuke shouted, "Haakon, we have to fight it together!"

"I'd rather die!" Haakon charged, right at Daisuke, again.

He knew the man wasn't an idiot, but right now he was certainly acting like one.

Daisuke waited until he was a few strides away, blasted the demon, then dodged, allowing its counterattack to run into Haakon, smashing him once more into a different section of wall.

Haakon got up again, slower this time.

"Sure you don't want to fight together?" Daisuke asked, never taking his eyes off the demon. Though vastly stronger, it was still as stupid as the weak demon that made up its core. That was a small favor.

"This one time only, I'll save your useless life," Haakon said. "Do you have a plan?"

"If you can keep it busy, it'll give me time to cast one of my stronger spells. That should weaken it enough for you to strike the final blow."

Haakon charged, the demon this time, his ax and armor undimmed.

As he did Daisuke began a spell of his own creation, a dark and potent spell that, if it worked as he planned, would rid him of two problems the same time.

V anessa kept to the shadows at the edge of the battle, careful to do nothing that might draw attention. Though if she was being honest, the giant demon was doing a fine job serving as a distraction. She doubted anyone would notice if she set off a fireball.

On the other side of the chamber, Haakon got slammed into a wall for the second time only to climb back to his feet unharmed. He was tough, she had to give him that. Teaming up with Daisuke might even be enough to defeat the demon. Only hopefully not too fast. Losing her distraction before she found and escaped with Razak's prison would be a problem.

Halfway around the altar chamber she spotted a door made to blend into the surrounding stone.

That looked promising.

She slipped through the door and followed an undecorated passage to yet another door, this one made of black wood and carved with the flaming skull of Abaddon.

She grinned. A promising find indeed. A quick check confirmed a lack of traps before a nudge pushed the door open, revealing an office filled with diabolist junk. Amulets, books and scrolls of all kinds littered every surface. None of it interested Vanessa. As an elementalist she had no use for these sorts of things.

The only thing of interest to her was Razak's prison. The problem was, she saw no sign of it. Everything here convinced her she'd found the Devil Man's private sanctum. The prison had to be here somewhere and she meant to find it.

Vanessa tossed aside papers, rifled through drawers that

creaked with protest, and discarded no-doubt-valuable trinkets without a second glance. The crashes and explosions from the altar chamber spurred her on.

Time was not on her side.

She turned her attention to an overfull bookshelf, its shelves straining under the weight of tomes and slate tablets. She tossed them aside one after the next, heedless of the occasional crunch of shattered stone.

Three shelves down she spotted a faint line. A flick of magic sliced the door apart revealing a hidden compartment. The item inside was a small bronze urn with a depression at the top featuring a unique rune.

Razak's prison at last.

Her moment of triumph was fleeting. Finding it was only half the battle. Now she had to escape.

Her only hope was that the Devil Man had another secret way out. He seemed like the untrusting type, so it wasn't beyond the realm of possibility.

She threw things aside with reckless abandon. Bookshelves toppled, the desk went over, and the carpet got tossed aside. And she found nothing.

When you had nowhere else to run, there was doubtless little point in having an emergency exit. This must've been the Devil Man's last redoubt.

With no other options, Vanessa sprinted back toward the battle. The corridor outside thrummed with the battle's ferocity, screams and roars reverberating off the walls.

She paused at the threshold of the altar chamber. Daisuke stood at the center of a dark circle, the Staff of Law raised above his head. The power swirling around him sent a shiver down her spine. Whatever spell he was casting, she was glad it wasn't pointed at her.

Haakon was busy hacking away at the demon, cutting grooves in its flesh but seeming to do no real damage. That was a shock. If there was one thing Haakon was good at, it was causing damage.

She put it all out of her mind. Only escape mattered now.

The Staff of Law was heavy in Daisuke's hands as he held it over his head. It felt like the power he'd gathered hung from the staff like weights on a barbell. Waves of darkness flashed in front of his eyes, momentarily blocking his view of Haakon's battle with the demon. The giant Norseman wasn't having much luck as the demon healed almost as quickly as he could carve it up. Rooting for Haakon felt strange, but when given the choice between a demon and a human, the decision was an easy one, even when the human was Haakon.

That the battle wasn't going very well didn't come as a huge surprise to Daisuke. The demon still crackled with power after its upgrade. On the plus side, its power diminished after each hit Haakon landed. If Erik's Helm lasted longer than the demon's aura, he might win.

The thought had barely crossed Daisuke's mind when the golden aura flickered.

The end wouldn't be far now.

Focusing even harder, Daisuke readied his spell. He had to unleash it at exactly the right moment.

Haakon landed a heavy blow, the golden ax burying itself deep in the demon's gut.

It roared and brought its fist down on Haakon, shattering his armor and smashing him to the floor. Its other hand swooped in, snatched him up before he could recover, and pulled him toward its mouth.

This was it.

Daisuke released the gathered energy right at Haakon. A black bolt hammered into the Norseman's back, mingling with his life force and making it unstable.

With a sharp gesture, Daisuke completed the spell.

An explosion of life force erupted from Haakon. His body vaporized, taking most of the demon's head and torso with him. The monster's legs still kicked feebly but soon they went still as well, before turning into black goo.

Daisuke's breath came in ragged gasps, the toll of the spell dragging him down to one knee. His whole body trembled from the exertion. If he never had to cast that spell again, it would be okay with him.

Out of the corner of his eye he spotted Helena staring at him, horrified. No surprise there. Using Haakon as a living bomb was kind of nasty, even if he was a psychotic murderer who would've happily killed them all.

Master, Vanessa has the prison and is attempting to sneak past you.

He swallowed a curse. After using a spell that strong, he was in no shape for a fight.

Tell Helena. Delay her, kill her, I don't care, just buy me some time.

Daisuke remained on his knee, careful to give no sign they'd spotted Vanessa. Given his weakness, he'd only have one chance to take her out. Assuming he chose the right moment to strike.

Getting him that moment would fall to Helena and Ruq.

CHAPTER NINETEEN

Helena's breath caught in her throat, the faint sound lost amidst the roar of battle. Daisuke, wrapped in swirling darkness, had transformed Haakon into a bomb. The explosion succeeded in destroying the demon, but the act was so cold-blooded she couldn't quite believe it. She'd thought, for however brief a time, Haakon was their ally. To use him the way he had seemed wrong.

A foolish thought no doubt, but an honest one. She wasn't sure how she felt about winning that way. On the other hand, being torn apart by an out-of-control demon didn't appeal to her at all.

Ruq's voice out of nowhere snapped her out of her indulgent thoughts. "Vanessa's making a run for it with the prison."

"Shit! Where?"

"Keep your voice down. Do you want to warn her that she's been spotted? She's invisible but you can see her outline to your right as she works her way around the perimeter of the chamber." Ruq kept his voice low. Now that the battle was over it seemed painfully quiet. "Daisuke's done for now. We need to buy him time to recover."

Helena's heart raced. She knew perfectly well that if she had to fight Vanessa on her own, she was screwed. Still, she should be able to buy a little time. Whether it would be enough for Daisuke to recover and back her up, only time would tell. Unless she wanted to let Vanessa flee with Razak's prison, there was no choice.

She silently cast a see invisible spell then shifted just enough to catch a glimpse of Vanessa as she crept ever closer to the door. The woman was focused on Daisuke who was still kneeling and taking deep breaths.

Helena would've been offended that she didn't warrant a glance, but after seeing what Daisuke did to Haakon, she couldn't blame Vanessa for focusing on him.

She could use that to her advantage.

Subtle but quick was the name of the game. Gather ether too quickly and Vanessa would be sure to sense it. But the risks grew the closer she got to the exit. Helena had to strike the right balance.

A few seconds later she was ready.

Helena spun and pointed, unleashing a golden blast at Vanessa.

The spell caught her off guard, hammering Vanessa into the wall and drawing a grunt of pain. Even better, she lost her grip on the prison and it went flying away from the door.

"No!" Vanessa shouted. A wave of her hand sent blue threads flying at Helena.

A barrier appeared but barely slowed the threads.

Helena dove out of the way, the passing heat searing her back.

So not good. She knew Vanessa was stronger than her but hadn't thought she was this much stronger.

"All you had to do was stay out of my way!" Vanessa screamed, enraged beyond all reason. "I didn't care about you! I only wanted the prison. But a simple win was too much to ask. Now I have to kill you."

Helena didn't like the crazy look in Vanessa's eyes. Whether the loss of her teammate or getting caught had pushed her into madness, Helena couldn't begin to guess, but something had broken in the woman.

When the fire threads came roaring in a second time, there were twice as many and they were thicker and hotter.

There was no way her barriers would stand up to them.

Helena ran for all she was worth. The fire threads gouged the floor and walls, barely missing Helena as they sought to slice her to ribbons.

If Daisuke didn't recover soon, she was going to end up as dead as Haakon.

A thread shot in at her only to divert at the last second when Vanessa screamed. Helena risked a glance that way and spotted Ruq flying back up toward the ceiling pursued by more of the fire threads. Much as she disliked the imp, it seemed Helena owed him her life.

Taking advantage of the distraction, Helena loosed a blast of her own. A golden fist slammed into Vanessa and hurled her halfway across the chamber to slide into the wall.

Vanessa climbed back to her feet, if possible looking even more pissed off than before. She glared at Helena as she looked around. It took a moment for Helena to realize that the prison was gone. Ruq must've hidden it during the chaos. Clever of him.

"Do you think you've stopped me?" Vanessa asked. "I

found it once and after I deal with you pests, I'll find it again."

Before she could cast, a black disk appeared under her feet and black lightning leapt out, arcing into her body and out her eyes and ears as her body spasmed.

Then she collapsed, steam rising from her corpse. Helena sensed no life force.

"Some of us pests are more difficult to deal with than others." Daisuke limped up beside her. "You okay?"

"I've been better, but I'm alive, thanks, to my considerable surprise, to Ruq."

"You always underestimate my greatness." Ruq soared down from the ceiling, Razak's prison in his little claws.

"Good work, both of you." Daisuke hobbled over to the chamber wall and slid to the floor.

"What now?" Helena asked.

"I'm too tired to shadow walk. I'm going to need at least half a day to recover my magic enough to take us home. My plan is to sit here and not move for at least a few hours. Then I'm going to search this dump for anything dangerous. Once I'm fully recovered, or near enough, we go home and tell the boss the good news. Not only do we have Razak's prison, but two members of the Blood of Solomon are dead. Difficult as it was, I can't deny this was a good day."

Helena slumped beside him. "I was shocked when you used that spell on Haakon. It felt wrong. It's stupid, I know, but he was fighting on our side and you betrayed him."

Daisuke snorted. "Are you seriously telling me you feel bad for that madman?"

"It's complicated. The way you used him felt dishonorable. Like it was worse than killing him in a straight-up fight."

Daisuke leaned his head back and closed his eyes. "Dead is dead and the world is better off without that piece of shit in it. If it makes you feel any better, there was no other way to beat the demon. The power boost raised it to a high level six. It would've killed us all."

Helena fell silent. There was nothing more to say. She wouldn't bring Haakon back even if she had the power to do so. The important thing was that they'd won, even if the victory felt dirty.

She turned to tell Daisuke that but found him sound asleep. With a little smile she rested her head on his shoulder and closed her eyes.

CHAPTER TWENTY

Daisuke woke slowly, his back aching from lying against the hard stone. On the plus side, his magic felt somewhat restored, though he wouldn't want to fight a major battle yet. In fact, he wouldn't want to do that for a couple more days at least, but he no longer felt on the verge of passing out so that was a win.

He glanced down and found Helena sound asleep beside him. He remembered her sitting down, but after that everything was blank.

"That's when you fell asleep." Ruq glided down from the ceiling.

"Shh, you'll wake her." Daisuke gingerly stood, careful not to jostle Helena.

Poor thing must have been really out of it. Almost getting killed would do that to you. Given how often it happened to him, almost dying no longer bothered Daisuke that much. He was pretty sure the technical term was exposure therapy. He smiled to himself and tried not to think too hard about what it said about his psyche.

They moved halfway across the chamber and Daisuke asked, "No trouble while we were out of it?"

"Nah, all quiet here. In fact, the barrier faded away about an hour ago. We can come and go as we please now."

Daisuke tried to grin but it made his face hurt. "We could if I was strong enough to shadow walk. As it stands, regular walking is about all I'm good for."

He shuffled over to Vanessa's body, using the Staff of Law like it was a walking stick. The black lightning had burned the life out of her, but didn't damage her body too much aside from a few scorch marks. Pity she was insane, Vanessa would've made a fine Circle agent.

A quick pat down of the body produced a fried cellphone and an antique-looking compass that, when he held it, didn't point north. It had some weak innate magic, but some artifacts only worked when you channeled ether into them. Out of curiosity, Daisuke did so.

The arrow pointed right at him.

"Guess we know how they found us," Ruq said. "Wonder how that thing works."

Daisuke shrugged, slipping the compass and cellphone into his satchel. "It'll be something for Donnie to play with when we get back. He should be able to sort it out in a hurry. If we're lucky, Crystal might be able to extract something from what's left of the cellphone."

"What are you going to do with her body?" Ruq asked.

"Disintegrate it I guess. I can't very well leave it intact in a place like this. Why?"

"I bet she'd make a good undead servant for you."

Daisuke groaned. "Give me a break. I'm not making any undead servants. Bad enough I have a demonic familiar."

"Hey!"

He left Vanessa's body for the moment and made his way over to Erik's Helm. Despite being in the center of the blast radius, the artifact didn't have a scratch on it. Much like the armor it generated, the helm appeared indestructible. Surely someone in the Circle would be able to make good use of the item.

"Where did Vanessa find the prison?" Daisuke asked.

"She came out a disguised door," Ruq said. "I didn't even see it until it opened."

"Hellpriests and giant demons tend to be distracting. Let's see what lies behind door number one."

Ruq glided over to the door. Even partway open it blended in well with the surrounding stone. Down a short hall and behind another door they found an office. A very messy office. In fact, if you'd told Daisuke a tornado had hit the room he wouldn't have doubted it. Vanessa had been very thorough in her search.

He was too tired to sift through the mess right now. "We'll have to come back and make a proper search later. Most likely all this crap will end up in the vault."

"Will that be before or after it ends up on our kitchen table?" Ruq asked.

"After, obviously."

Leaving the mess behind, Daisuke retraced his steps to the altar chamber just in time to see Helena sit up and yawn.

"Hey. Have a nice nap?" Daisuke asked.

"Yeah, though I didn't think you'd wake up before I did. How are you feeling?"

"Much better, though nowhere near a hundred percent." He summoned his trunk, popped it open and pulled out two MREs. Far from his preferred meal, they were still about four thousand calories each and right now he needed energy.

After their visit to Australia, Daisuke had added a week's worth of food to his supplies. He refused to get caught without resources again.

He tossed one of the packages to Helena, who caught it and tore it open. "Thanks."

They ate in silence for a while before she asked, "What now?"

"I'm nearly recovered enough to take us home." Daisuke chewed quickly, trying his best not to taste the so-called food. "We make our report, then I think a day of rest would be in order, then I'll come back and collect all the magic odds and ends we found in the Devil Man's office. Once that's done, I think we can call this mission finished."

"Agreed." Helena swallowed a final mouthful then offered him her leftovers, which he took without comment. "Did you free Remi?"

"Not yet. He knows a lot more than just where to find this place. I mean to wring every secret he's hiding out of him. At a minimum he knows which gangs still have pet demons. Those will need to be dealt with sooner rather than later.

She made a face, but didn't comment.

"If you've got something on your mind, say it."

"It just seems wrong, keeping someone's soul imprisoned. If he was alive and in jail I wouldn't give it a second thought, but souls are different, special, I guess."

"They are different," Daisuke agreed. "It's much harder for a soul to lie to me. That makes them better sources of information than the living. Given where Remi is likely to end up, I doubt he's anxious to be freed."

Daisuke stood, tossed Erik's Helm in his trunk along with

Razak's prison, and put it away. When Helena joined him, he scooped her up and stepped into the nearest shadow.

I t was with tremendous relief that Daisuke completed his report. He hadn't left much out beyond his plan to read the Devil Man's occult collection before he turned it in. On the desk in front of him sat Erik's Helm, the cellphone, and the compass that somehow always pointed to him. Daisuke saw no particular value in any of them, at least for himself, and was happy to hand them over.

The boss leaned back in her chair and pursed her lips. The thoughtful pose was nothing unusual for her. At last, she said, "Well done, both of you. This mission eliminated a number of threats and I couldn't be more pleased. I'll be sure to scratch Vanessa and Haakon's names off the list of Blood agents. You've both earned a long rest, probably a longer one than you're going to get. I'll take Razak's prison to the vault later. Having a quarter of the greater demons locked up is a relief."

Daisuke nodded. "Is Jinx cleared for fieldwork?"

"She has one more day, though as far as I can tell she's fully recovered and Rin agrees. I may have to adjust the protocol further for her. Four days might be enough for a half demon."

Helena hadn't said a word during the debriefing. Daisuke assumed she was still upset about the way he dealt with Haakon. That didn't overly bother him. Much as he liked Helena, he refused to be bound by her ideals. Doing so would be like fighting with one hand tied behind his back.

"I'm heading home by way of Stein's Bakery. Care to join me for some sugary indulgence?"

Helena shook her head. "I'm still full from the MRE. I think I'll just chill at home, maybe read a book."

"Sure." Daisuke stood. "See you later. You too, boss."

He slipped out of the office and nearly ran into Jinx, who was waiting outside. Daisuke closed the door and cocked his head. "What's up?"

"I sensed you arrive via the shadow paths. Vixen is awake and she asked to speak with you when you had time. Is now okay?"

"We should buy our sweets first," Ruq said.

"The bakery isn't going anywhere. I don't mind talking with her now. Do you know what she wants?"

Jinx shook her head. "Her strength is returning slowly but surely and Rin thinks she'll be ready to walk around a bit in a day or two. From the little she's told me, I doubt she's got anywhere to go once she's better. Maybe that's what she wants to discuss."

Daisuke grinned. "One way to find out. Let's ask her."

When Daisuke had gone the boss asked, "Something else on your mind?"

Helena wasn't sure how to express what she was feeling. Some of the things she'd seen Daisuke do on this mission left her troubled. That he in turn seemed untroubled by them to the point that he reported all the details during the debriefing bothered her almost as much as the acts themselves.

"I've been doing fieldwork for a few years now. I've been

in fights and seen people die. I've even killed when there was no other choice. But what Daisuke did, first with Remi's soul, then Haakon…" She shook her head. "I don't know what to think."

"As best I can tell, he did what was necessary to complete the mission. While I don't condone, as a general rule, interfering with a soul's final journey, sometimes circumstances force questionable acts. I'll never question a field agent's decisions unless they were truly egregious. Daisuke's weren't, not in my eyes. Jinx will be ready to resume her role as Daisuke's partner starting tomorrow. If working with him is going to be a problem, I can arrange for you not to."

That blunt statement made Helena's stomach knot up. Did what happened really change how she felt about Daisuke? She couldn't say for sure and it bothered her.

"I don't know," Helena said. "I guess I need more time to process everything."

"Take it," the boss said. "I have nothing for you or Daisuke at the moment. You've earned some time off."

"Thanks, boss. Not just for the time off, but letting me vent. I know it's not very professional."

When the boss smiled at Helena, it felt like golden light shone out of her. "That's what I'm here for. Never think I don't appreciate all the things you and the other Circle members do. You've all chosen an incredibly difficult path through life. If I can make that path a little easier, I'm happy to do so."

Helena stood and left the office. A trip to the library always made her feel better. She'd pick up a new novel and read it in a nice hot bubble bath.

Some of the worry gone, she left the shop behind and headed for home.

D aisuke marched up the stairs to the second-floor recovery room ahead of Jinx. The door to Vixen's room was open, but he knocked anyway before stepping inside.

Vixen was sitting up in her bed, a white robe wrapped around her. It made a stark contrast to her red hair. He hadn't noticed it before, but she had a dusting of freckles across her cheeks. They made her look young.

"Hey." Daisuke sat beside the bed so as not to loom over her. "You're looking way better than the last time I saw you. What's on your mind?"

Vixen looked away from him, clearly not sure how to begin. Daisuke remained silent, letting her gather her thoughts. Given everything she'd been through, her hesitation didn't surprise him.

After half a minute she turned to face him. "Thank you for saving me. After all I've done, I'm not sure I deserved saving, but I am grateful all the same."

Vixen offered a little bow which made him smile. She was no more Japanese than he was a Spaniard, but that was exactly what someone from there would've done and it made him nostalgic.

"I was happy to do it. Whatever you feel about your past, try to remember it was the spirit bound to your body that made you do it. You had no choice in the matter. Also, Remi and the Devil Man are dead, so you have nothing to fear from them."

Her green eyes got very wide. "Dead? Both of them? But they were so strong. What happened?"

Daisuke debated not telling her the gory details for a

moment but Vixen deserved to know the truth. "I killed Remi and Abaddon turned against the Devil Man, claiming his soul in the process. Neither of them was a great loss to the world. If you're worried about those two doing something to you, don't."

She sagged with relief and her lower lip started to tremble. He hoped she didn't start crying.

Lucky for him she recovered herself before that happened. "Thank you for telling me. I've been so afraid since I woke up. Knowing they're gone takes a weight off my mind. Now I just have to figure out what I'm going to do next. I have no family or friends. I mean old friends; Jinx has been lovely these last couple days."

Out of the corner of his eye Daisuke saw Jinx's pale skin flush at the compliment.

"Anyway, I have no home or place to go. I can't even remember how to fight now that the spirit is gone."

"I've been thinking about your situation," Daisuke said. "One of the shop girls is getting married next month. She's also four months pregnant. She gave her two weeks' notice and we need to find a replacement. You already know the shop's secret, so if you're interested, I'll bet I can convince the boss to hire you. Finding you a studio apartment in our building should be easy too. I know the owner. It's just a thought, but if you're interested let me know."

Now she did start crying. "Why are you doing all this for me? I tried to kill you not that long ago. I'm a stranger. You owe me nothing, yet you saved my life and now you're offering to help me rebuild my life. Why?"

"My job," Daisuke said, "is dark and ugly. I hunt and kill monsters that most people don't want to think about. Plenty of those monsters are human rather than demon. My preference is helping people rather than killing them. So when I see the chance to pull someone out of a bad situation, I do. You've had a rough go. I won't pretend to understand everything you went through before we met, but you've got a second chance. I'd like to help you make the most of it."

"Me too," Jinx added.

"I don't think I'm worthy of your kindness, but I will try to be."

Daisuke stood and squeezed Vixen's shoulder. "Right now, all you need to do is get better. All that stuff I said, it'll be here when you're ready. If you want, I can check in on you again another time."

Vixen nodded. "I'd like that, thank you."

He offered his most reassuring smile and turned toward the door. Jinx fell in beside him.

At the top of the staircase she said, "That was very thoughtful of you. It reminded me of when we first met."

"Sometimes people just need a friend. I'm happy to be one for both you and Vixen. Now, I can hear Ruq's stomach grumbling so I'd best get to the bakery. Want to come?"

"I'm not hungry yet," Jinx said. "Maybe breakfast tomorrow?"

"You're on."

Jinx kissed his cheek and Daisuke took his leave. All things considered, despite the difficulties he'd faced on this mission, he was pleased with the results. Pity all his jobs couldn't end equally well.

AUTHOR NOTE

Hello everyone,

Well, Daisuke's battle with the Cult of Abaddon has reached its conclusion with both he and his friends still in one piece. Not a bad result considering what they were up against.

But don't think our hero is out of the woods yet. Plenty of demon prisons remain to be found and The Blood of Solomon aren't the sorts to take their losses lightly.

I hope you'll join me when the next book comes out. To be the first to find out when that will be, you can sign up for my newsletter at www.jamesewisher.com.

As always, thanks for reading.

James E Wisher

ALSO BY JAMES E. WISHER

The 72 Demons

The Blood of Solomon

A Friend in Need

The Demon Masks

Hunt For The Devil Man

The Immortal Apprentice Trilogy

The War With Audin (Prequel Novella)

The Hunt For Revenge

The Army of Darkness

The Apprentice Reborn

The Soul Bound Saga

An Unwelcome Journey

Darkness in Tiber

Depths of Betrayal

The Black Iron Empire

Overmage

The Divine Key Trilogy

Shadow Magic

For The Greater Good

The Divine Key Awakens

The Portal Wars Saga

The Hidden Tower

The Great Northern War

The Portal Thieves

The Master of Magic

The Chamber of Eternity

The Heart of Alchemy

The Sanguine Scroll

Shadow of The Dragons

The Dragonspire Chronicles

The Black Egg

The Mysterious Coin

The Dragons' Graveyard

The Slave War

The Sunken Tower

The Dragon Empress

The Dragonspire Chronicles Omnibus Vol. 1

The Dragonspire Chronicles Omnibus Vol. 2

The Complete Dragonspire Chronicles Omnibus

Soul Force Saga

Disciples of the Horned One Trilogy:

Darkness Rising

Raging Sea and Trembling Earth

Harvest of Souls

Disciples of the Horned One Omnibus

Chains of the Fallen Arc:

Dreaming in the Dark

On Blackened Wings

Chains of the Fallen Omnibus

The Complete Soul Force Saga Omnibus

The Aegis of Merlin:

The Impossible Wizard

The Awakening

The Chimera Jar

The Raven's Shadow

Escape From the Dragon Czar

Wrath of the Dragon Czar

The Four Nations Tournament

Death Incarnate

Atlantis Rising

Rise of the Demon Lords

The Pale Princess

Malice

Aegis of Merlin Omnibus Vol 1.

Aegis of Merlin Omnibus Vol 2.

The Complete Aegis of Merlin Omnibus

Other Fantasy Novels:

The Squire

Death and Honor Omnibus

The Rogue Star Series:

Children of Darkness

Children of the Void

Children of Junk

Rogue Star Omnibus Vol. 1

Children of the Black Ship

Children of The End

ABOUT THE AUTHOR

James E. Wisher is a writer of science fiction and Fantasy novels. He's been writing since high school and reading everything he could get his hands on for as long as he can remember.

f **▶** **BB** **a**

9 781685 200862